Sherlock Holmes – The Baker Street Archive

Another collection of previously unknown cases from the extraordinary career of Mr. Sherlock Holmes

Mark Mower

First edition published in 2022

© Copyright 2022 Mark Mower

The right of Mark Mower to be identified as the author of this work has been asserted by him in accordance with the Copyright, Designs and Patents Act 1998.

All rights reserved. No reproduction, copy or transmission of this publication may be made without express prior written permission. No paragraph of this publication may be reproduced, copied or transmitted except with express prior written permission or in accordance with the provisions of the Copyright Act 1956 (as amended). Any person who commits any unauthorised act in relation to this publication may be liable to criminal prosecution and civil claims for damage.

All characters appearing in this work are fictitious or used fictitiously. Except for certain historical personages, any resemblance to real persons, living or dead, is purely coincidental. The opinions expressed herein are those of the author and not of MX Publishing.

Hardcover ISBN 9781804240434
Paperback ISBN 9781804240441
AUK ePub ISBN 9781804240458
AUK PDF ISBN 9781804240465

Published in the UK by MX Publishing
335 Princess Park Manor, Royal Drive,
London, N11 3GX
www.mxpublishing.co.uk
Cover design by Brian Belanger

Contents

Preface		4
1.	A Diplomatic Affair	6
2.	The Neckar Reawakening	20
3.	The Yuletide Heist	60
4.	The Case of the SS Bokhara	96
5.	The Misadventure of the Norfolk Poacher	105
6.	The Case of the Learned Linguist	143
About the Author		175
Copyright Information		176

Preface

Dear readers – I had imagined that the book I released last year, titled *Sherlock Holmes: The Baker Street Epilogue*, would serve as the final volume of previously unknown Holmes and Watson cases from the prized collection of stories I inherited from my uncle in 1939. But I am pleased to say that is not the case. The response to the book has been so overwhelming that I have been encouraged to select yet more tales which might excite the interests of readers across the globe. I trust you will embrace this new volume as positively as you did for the four earlier books.

It is an irrefutable fact that Sherlock Holmes was a pioneer in all aspects of crime detection and investigation, including a myriad of sciences allied to his craft. From forensics and graphology to ballistics and toxicology, he was a gifted exponent of them all. Yesterday, we saw the publication of an academic paper titled the *Molecular Structure of Nucleic Acids: A Structure for Deoxyribose Nucleic Acid* by Francis Crick and James D. Watson (*no relative, as far as I'm aware!*). The authors are the first to describe the double helix structure of DNA, the molecule containing human genes. I know that if Holmes were still alive, he would have marvelled at this research and pondered how the discovery might further *the science of deduction.*

There is clearly no loss of appetite when it comes to new Sherlock Holmes stories, so I am pleased to present six more previously overlooked gems which neatly illustrate his deductive capabilities. From the seemingly supernatural challenge of *The Neckar Reawakening* to the seasonal conundrum of *The Yuletide Heist*, there is much to entertain and enthral us.

So, as you have done before, dim the gas lamp, get settled in your favourite wing-backed chair, and steady yourself with another glass of your favourite tipple. For it promises to be a reassuringly long night. And, as always, *"The game is afoot!"*

Christopher Henry Watson, MD

Bexley Heath, Kent – 26th April 1953

1. A Diplomatic Affair

We live in extraordinary times, Watson," said Holmes, placing his folded newspaper down on the table and stepping over to the window. "An American President assassinated, and his killer sentenced to death. Charles Guiteau's insanity plea was never likely to succeed in saving him from execution, yet the man is clearly of unsound mind. A senseless act – and all because he believed he had played some small part in James Garfield's election victory and expected to be rewarded with an ambassadorial post. That a president can be slain at close quarters by a handgun in a railway station should give us all pause for thought. Is anyone really safe from the murderous intentions of a disturbed and determined assassin?"

I too had been shocked to hear the news of President Garfield's untimely demise the previous year and the recent trial of his murderer, but there was something about Holmes's very pointed remarks which sat uneasily with me. "Am I to take it that you are fearful for your own safety?"

"No, just alive to the possibilities. By its nature, my work brings me into contact with all manner of criminals, including hired killers. We must therefore be ever vigilant. So when I see an advertisement placed in the *Pall Mall Gazette* inviting assassins to act, you will appreciate why I say we live in extraordinary times. "See what you make of it."

He turned back to the table, picked up the newspaper and passed it to me, pointing at the piece in question with the long stem of his churchwarden. The advertisement ran as follows:

Notice

We gladly postponed tonight's dietary binge, so hold onto fried nightingales.

SEFTEN

I read the piece three times before looking back towards Holmes with an expression of some confusion. "I can see no obvious threat. I'll grant you that the wording is cryptic, but why do you believe it to have a more sinister meaning?"

He reached for his favourite ink pen and took the paper back, laying it on the table once more and folding the broadsheet into a more manageable size. "I make it my job to scrutinise any odd notices that appear in the London press. It is often the means by which the criminal fraternity broadcasts its intentions." He began to underline odd letters in the notice, before placing the newspaper back in my lap. "Is that any clearer?"

I looked again at the print, casting my eyes over the underlined words, but was still unable to discern any particular meaning.

Notice

<u>We</u> gladly po<u>st</u>pon<u>e</u>d tonight's <u>di</u>etary bi<u>n</u>ge, <u>so hold onto</u> <u>fri</u>ed <u>night</u>ingales.

SEF<u>TEN</u>

Holmes eyed me with mock disgruntlement. "Come on, Watson! Do I have to spell it out? Consider just the underlined words. Is it not clear that the hidden message reads: 'WE Gladstone to die in Soho on Fri night'?"

I studied the paper afresh, seeing for the first time that my colleague was absolutely correct. The message did appear to be forecasting the death of the Prime Minister, William Ewart Gladstone. "How did you identify this? I asked.

"I have trained myself to examine seemingly nonsensical advertisements in order to see what is buried within. With my experience, identifying this message was elementary."

"But why are the four central letters of '*SEFTEN*' underlined as well?"

"That may very well point us in the direction of the author. If I remember rightly, the rallying cry of the Egyptian rebels in the mutiny of 1879 was 'Egypt for the Egyptians!' The initial letters spell out '*EFTE*'."

"That is astonishing," I cried, remembering that it had been reported in the papers only a day earlier that on Sunday, 8th January, Britain and France had delivered a joint declaration to the Egyptian government guaranteeing the autocracy of Mohammad Tewfik Pasha, the Khedive of Egypt. "So this may be a plot linked to the hostility around Britain's continued support for the Khedival regime in Cairo, in opposition to those who are calling for constitutional government?"

"That is entirely possible. Although my knowledge of international affairs in that part of the world is not as good as it could be. Luckily, I have an exceptional contact within Whitehall who can provide us with a comprehensive analysis of any threats posed by Colonel Urabi and his military faction."

With no further explanation Holmes announced that there was little time to waste. If the apparent threat to our Prime Minister was to be believed, we had but two days until his predicted death. Donning coats, scarves, and hats, we set off hastily from 221B in the direction of Whitehall.

****

It was exceptionally cold out on the street, the result of the rising air pressure which had gripped the country since the start of the year. While bright, the sky had assumed a pinkish hue, hinting at the possibility of further snow. I was thankful for the thick woollen muffler which sat beneath my chin – a Christmas gift from the ever-thoughtful Mrs. Hudson.

We hailed a passing hansom on Orchard Street as the icy wind continued to bite, the cabbie taking us on a circuitous route through Grosvenor Square and Mayfair, before heading off along a myriad of small thoroughfares I did not recognise. Holmes seemed strangely quiet in the cab and markedly reluctant to say any more about his well-placed contact, beyond stressing that "in any matters of information or intelligence across government, this man has no equal."

It was close to eleven o'clock that morning when the hansom finally came to a halt outside the grand white façade of a government building in Whitehall. Having paid the cabbie, Holmes waved him off before heading briskly towards the entrance. It was only when we were stood within the spacious foyer of the interior, before an imposing marble staircase, that he spoke again. "Watson, it is not my intention to offend you, but you really must believe me when I say it is in everyone's best interests that I meet with my contact alone. I trust you will not mind waiting here for the short time it will take?"

While the pronouncement took me by surprise, I was not in the least bit affronted, trusting, as I always did, in the absolute integrity of my colleague's reasoning. As it transpired, I had but little time to sit, for it took Holmes less than twenty minutes to conclude his business. Shortly afterwards we were once again within the interior of a cab, this time heading towards Knightsbridge. The only additional information he would furnish was that we would be meeting with "an important French diplomat."

Holmes now seemed more favourably disposed to discuss the nature of his enquiries back in Whitehall. "This affair appears to be far more complex than I first imagined." He paused to pull up the collar on his long overcoat and shivered momentarily. "My contact was pleased to discuss the coded notice, which he had himself already spotted. As a result, he has commissioned us to take further action. You'll be pleased to learn that we are now acting as unofficial diplomats for the British Government!"

"Really?" I said, bemused.

"Yes. It seems we were right to suppose that there may be some Egyptian link to this apparent threat to the Prime Minister. As you know, the nationalists within that country have been rallying behind their leader, Colonel Ahmed Urabi, since the uprising of 1879. In a bid to quell the revolutionary tendencies of the nationalists, Khedive Tewfik invited Urabi to join his cabinet. Since that time, Urabi has been reforming Egypt's military, financial and civic institutions in a bid to weaken the Anglo-French domination of the Khedival administration. You might remember that since 1876 – when the Khedivate was effectively declared bankrupt – both countries have assumed a shared control over Egypt's economic affairs."

"So Whitehall might have good reason to suspect that any attempt to assassinate Gladstone might be part of this resistance to Britain's foreign policy?"

"Indeed. Although in this case, I believe that the coded notice is merely purporting to be a death threat from the Egyptian nationalists. My contact also believes that to be the case and is keen for us to pursue that line of enquiry."

"I'm not sure I understand."

"Well, consider the nature and placement of the communication. The notice appeared in the liberal *Pall Mall Gazette*. Only those within government, or in close diplomatic circles, are likely to know that the publication is our Prime Minister's favourite. The 'EFTE' sign off within the name 'Seften' is a little too obvious and twee – particularly as it is written in English. Most assassins tend to leave their calling card *after* they have acted, not before. Their biggest fear is being discovered before they are able to complete their task."

I could see the logic of Holmes's reasoning but raised one small objection. "Yes, but the would-be assassin also pointed to the likely location of the killing. Perhaps he is brazen enough to announce his intentions before acting and confident in his assertion that Soho will be the place where he can achieve his objective."

"A fair point, Watson – and one which I did consider. But my contact has assured me that Gladstone has no planned engagements in Soho, or indeed anywhere in London, on Friday evening."

"So that part of the communication was a red herring then?"

"Not as such. He believes that its inclusion was deliberate. In fact, he went further in postulating that it was something of a private joke at the Prime Minister's expense. In earlier years, as part of his evangelical sensibilities, Gladstone was often to be found walking the streets of Soho undertaking 'rescue' work with ladies of ill-repute. There has always been more than a whiff of suspicion about this supposed moral crusade."

I found myself more confused than ever. "But if the missive was not written by an Egyptian nationalist and poses no real threat, are you suggesting that it is, in fact, part of some elaborate hoax?"

"Far from it – the placement of the notice is a calculated act of brinkmanship and international diplomacy. I had my suspicions, but the trip to Whitehall convinced me that I was on the right track. Let us consider the position that Gladstone finds himself in. On the one hand, it is a matter of prestige that he wishes to retain Britain's influence over Egypt and preserve the Suez Canal route to India. On the other, he has, thus far, pursued a liberal non-interventionist approach, believing that if armed intercession is necessary, this should be the responsibility of the Turkish Sultan as *Suzerain* for the region. By attempting to posit the notion that Gladstone should fear assassination by the Egyptian nationalists, the author is really sending the message that our government should act more directly in suppressing the threat to the *status quo* in Egypt."

I began to comprehend his meaning. "That being the case, there is only one country likely to want to push us into such an undertaking. I understand now why we are planning to meet with a French diplomat."

"Exactly. France is keen for Britain to honour its *entente* commitments and intervene more directly to suppress the nationalist threat. Its government is also resolutely hostile to the idea of Turkish intervention in Egypt, or, indeed, the interference of any other powers."

Our cab had, by this time, reached an impressive building at 58 Knightsbridge, close to Albert Gate and one of the entrances to Hyde Park. A light flurry of snow had begun to fall and looked as if it might settle. As we approached the building, I had a final question: "Who is it we are about to see?"

He looked at me and smiled broadly. My contact has informed me that the former Prime Minister of France, Charles de Freycinet, is currently residing in the building and would be receptive to a visit. Our impending arrival should already have been communicated by telegraph. While we have no official capacity to act, I have been asked to investigate whether there is any evidence to support the notion that the coded message was placed deliberately by an agent working for the French government."

"That will not be easy to ascertain," I replied.

"We will see, my friend."

Some five minutes later we were being shown into one of the large suites housed within the top floor of the five-storey building. It was luxurious in both size and decoration and looked more like the interior of a French château than a London residence. A man stepped out from behind a large and ornate desk set before one of the windows overlooking Hyde Park. He was slim and elegant, dressed in an immaculately tailored black jacket, beneath which he wore a red velvet waistcoat and matching bow tie. His full beard and moustache, along with the hair to the sides of his thinning scalp, were as white as any I had ever seen, and lent him a striking, statesman-like, appearance. He approached us with a warm smile and shook each of us by the hand with an iron-like grip.

"Gentlemen, you are indeed welcome. Please take a seat." His English was impeccable and the timbre of his voice low and melodious. I noticed that he seemed to be studying Holmes very intently as we took to our seats. "So, you are *Sherlock* Holmes?" he said, more by way of observation than enquiry.

Holmes nodded, "Yes, and this is my close colleague, Dr. John Watson."

"Well, it is a pleasure to meet you. Now, may I offer you some refreshment?" He pointed towards a baroque side-table, on which sat a large selection of wines and spirits. "Perhaps a glass of port, some Madeira wine, or maybe a small measure of Vin Mariani?"

I winced at the mention of the latter, knowing full-well that the lively mixture of Bordeaux wine and cocaine within the popular tonic had hastened the demise of many a poet, politician, and pope. While I opted for a small glass of sherry, Holmes surprised me by readily accepting a glass of the intoxicating cocktail.

We spent some minutes talking about de Freycinet's background before he entered politics. He had grown up in the southwest of France and had later studied engineering at the École Polytechnique in Paris. When he mentioned that he had undertaken several scientific missions, including one to the United Kingdom, Holmes announced equably that he knew of the work: "A most competent study, sir. I recollect the notable paper you published in 1867, the '*Mémoire sur le travail des femmes et des enfants dans les manufactures de l'Angleterre.*'" Our host looked incredulous. I could but marvel at his pronunciation. To that point, I had been unaware that Holmes could speak any French.

Our conversation moved on to a general discussion about European affairs and the growing influence of both Germany and Russia. We agreed that the *entente* between our two great nations was essential in protecting Anglo-French interests across the globe. It was at this point that Holmes directed the dialogue more specifically towards the subject of Egypt. This prompted something of a snigger from de Freycinet.

"Tut, tut, Mr. Holmes. You have let your guard down. I was curious to know the real reason for your visit, and now you have revealed it. I am taking it that Whitehall is keen to know how I might view the possibility of military intervention in that country. Would that be a fair summary?"

Holmes did not deny that Egypt was indeed the matter we wished to discuss.

"Why would my views be of interest to your handler back in Whitehall?" he then asked.

I saw a flash of annoyance cross my colleague's face. He prided himself on being the most unique of private enquiry agents, and I knew that the reference to a *handler* had rankled him. Regaining his composure, he replied: "I know that you resigned your position as Prime Minister in September 1880, but since that time you have continued to operate in the highest of diplomatic circles. In particular, you have been something of a trusted confidante for certain officials within the British government. Our soon to be announced 'Foreign Intelligence Committee' is well aware that you are likely to be reinstated as Prime Minister by the end of this month, and your portfolio of responsibilities will include that of Foreign Minister. So your views on the Egyptian dilemma are of particular interest to Whitehall."

The Frenchman leaned forward and reached for a wooden box that sat on the front of his desk and offered up the contents to us. Holmes and I both took one of the long Panamanian cigars and watched as de Freycinet did the same. It was only when all three cigars had been lit, that our host responded.

"Gentlemen, since you have seen fit to disclose such a sensitive piece of information, I will be candid with you also. Barring some unforeseen calamity on the sea-crossing back to France, I do expect to be asked by the president to take up my former position within a matter of weeks. As for my views on the Egyptian debacle, I believe strongly that some form of direct military intervention is now needed to put a stop to the ambitions of the nationalists and remove the threat posed by Colonel Urabi and his supporters. I would also prefer not to let Turkey gain any foothold within the country. It is a concern to me that Prime Minister Gladstone does not appear to share my enthusiasm for such an undertaking."

Holmes reached inside his jacket and retrieved the folded pages of the *Pall Mall Gazette* from an inside pocket. He laid the notice with its underscored message on de Freycinet's desk and looked directly at him. "Is that why you placed this coded despatch in today's newspaper?"

"Mon Dieu! Why would you believe that I wrote this communiqué?"

"Observation and supposition. I imagine that the construction of such a cipher would appeal to you personally and play to your talents. You are a gifted engineer by profession, with a mastery of mathematics and strong skills in both organisation and problem solving – credentials which helped to secure your election to the prestigious Academy of Sciences. Your English language skills are first-rate, and through your diplomatic work you have become well-versed in the art of communication and subterfuge. In your position, you are likely to know that the *Pall Mall Gazette* is

Gladstone's preferred daily newspaper and be aware of the intimations concerning his night-time activities in Soho."

Charles de Freycinet laughed with some gusto. "That is some supposition, sir! But do you have any evidence for your assertion?" He said this playfully, as if the whole exchange were nothing more than a parlour game.

"I have two small, but telling, observations which lend weight to my hypothesis. Firstly, there is a discarded copy of the *Pall Mall Gazette* in the wastebasket to your side. That it is opened to the exact same page as this advertisement cannot be a coincidence. More tellingly, the ink blotter on your desk testifies to your recent word games. While it is covered in a multitude of random jottings in both French and English, there are three words in the top right corner which tell their own story. You have written down both 'dietary' and 'dietery', suggesting that you were initially unsure how to spell the word *dietary*. And beside them, is the single word 'rossignol' – a translation of the English *nightingale*."

"I see I have significantly underestimated your talents, Mr. Holmes. And I must concede that you have outflanked me on this occasion. I did indeed compose the notice. It is not the first time I have used the London press to send a covert message imploring your government to change its foreign policy. Of course, I would never admit publicly to doing so."

Ever the diplomat, he said this as if seeking confirmation that the matter would not be talked of afterwards. Holmes responded accordingly. "You may rest assured that I will never disclose your role in this affair." *

"That is kind of you. Of course, my bigger concern is whether I can genuinely persuade your government to change its stance on Egypt and back the idea of joint intervention."

I was surprised by Holmes's response. "Given that we are speaking openly of matters which are not to be made public, I can share with you the views of my contact in Whitehall. He is of the opinion that the machinery of government will operate so as to force Gladstone's hand. It is only a matter of time before the Prime Minister will be pushed to lay aside his pacifist inclinations and authorise some form of British military intervention in Egypt. He suggests only that you hold your nerve until that time has come."

It was a most astonishing disclosure and I could but wonder at the ramifications of communicating this to the French at that time.

Our meeting ended not long after this, with de Freycinet thanking Holmes for his intercession and indicating that it would do much to preserve the diplomatic bonds between our two countries. We left Knightsbridge as heavy snow began to fall on the capital. I hoped it was not a portent of things to come.

It was only later in the year that I was to realise just how significant our meeting that day had been in shaping world events. On Monday, 30th January, Charles de Freycinet was reinstated as Prime Minister, with additional responsibilities as the Foreign Secretary of France. He continued to press Britain to take a more direct approach in unseating the nationalists within Egypt. And despite the pacifist proclamations of the Gladstone administration, the country was to become embroiled in the Anglo-Egyptian War after the bombardment of the city of Alexandria in the July of 1882.

Holmes seemed content to downplay his involvement in the affair. His view was that the political and military events which unfolded at that time were largely predictable given the power and influence of certain officials within Whitehall. And it is only now, with the benefit of hindsight that I can begin to understand exactly what he meant. While assisting Holmes on the 1888 case I recorded as *The Greek Interpreter*, I realised of course that his mysterious governmental contact was none other than his older brother, Mycroft Holmes.

*Note: This was something of a smokescreen, for Holmes's words did not prevent me from writing up the narrative which I now set before you. It was out of respect for Charles de Freycinet that I have waited a great many years before finally committing the story to paper. The French statesman and four times Prime Minister of the Third Republic died last week, on Monday, 14th May 1923 – JHW.

2. The Neckar Reawakening

The March of 1895 proved to be a busy month for Mr. Sherlock Holmes, engaged as he was on four significant criminal cases and several other puzzling conundrums. From the notes I kept at the time, I recollect that the most memorable of these was the troubling matter of *The Neckar Reawakening*. The narrative which follows serves to illustrate the nature of this peculiar affair.

It was close to nine o'clock that morning – a bright, sunny day which promised to continue the run of fine weather we had been experiencing for well over a week. While I sat at the table of our Baker Street apartment drinking coffee and reading the newspapers, Holmes was seated in his favourite armchair close to the hearth going through all the correspondence which Mrs. Hudson had delivered to him not five minutes earlier.

"It seems we are once again in demand," said he, leaning forward and tapping out the ashes of his after-breakfast pipe. "A telegram from our old friend Captain George Drummond. He has something of a mystery on his hands and asks for our assistance. How do you fancy a trip to the countryside, Watson?"

I could not disguise my enthusiasm. "Sounds splendid! It must be a good five or six years since we last met up with Drummond. I take it that he's still Chief Constable of the West Sussex force?"

"Yes. And a very astute and likeable chap if my memory serves. While he has provided no further details, I feel certain that this will be no run-of-the-mill investigation, so will happily oblige him."

He reached for his pocket watch and for a moment was lost in his own thoughts, before then springing from the chair with some vigour. "If we set off smartly, we can reach Arundel before lunchtime. I'll ask young Billy to despatch a telegram to Drummond confirming that we are on our way. And it may be as well to pack an overnight bag before heading to London Bridge. Will your practice schedule allow for such a trip?"

In truth I had little medical work at that time to dissuade me. So it was that within fifteen minutes of his pronouncement, Holmes and I were heading by cab towards the station for a scenic excursion on the London, Brighton, and South Coast Railway.

Some ten minutes beyond midday, our train pulled into Arundel station where we disembarked. There was a light breeze and the steam from the idling locomotive billowed back along the platform in thick grey clouds. Waiting for us on the station concourse was a police dog cart and a large bay-coloured horse, besides which stood a tall, fair-haired, officer in a serge uniform with a high collar. He introduced himself as Police Constable Colin Daubney and smiled with some familiarity as he held out his hand to greet the two of us in turn. "It's an honour to meet you both again, gentlemen. I was but a newly recruited probationer when you were last here helping with the strange case of Colonel Warburton's madness."

"Indeed," said Holmes, "and I seem to remember that you were instrumental in finding the Colonel's missing cufflink, which proved to be a crucial piece of evidence in helping us to solve the case. The pleasure is all mine, Constable."

The officer flushed and seemed momentarily lost for words. I intervened, sensing his discomfort, being unsurprised that Holmes should remember such a detail: "Where are you taking us? Are we to meet with the Chief Constable?"

Daubney nodded and beckoned for us to step up into the cart. "Yes, Captain Drummond is in Binsted, a little over two miles from here. Knowing your methods, Mr. Holmes, he was keen for you to see where the body was found."

"So, it's death we're concerned with. In his telegram, Drummond gave no indication as to the nature of the case. Is there anything further you can tell us?"

"Certainly. The body of a young woman was discovered early this morning in a pond on the outskirts of the village. At first, we believed she might have drowned, or had taken her own life. But when Sergeant Cotter and I retrieved the body from the water, we knew there was more to it."

My friend's interest was piqued. "Why was that?"

"The body showed no signs of any struggle. We could see no obvious wounds or bruising to the head, chest, arms or legs of the poor girl, and her hands were lily white with no dirt beneath the fingernails. She was wearing only a thin, white, cotton shift, with nothing on her legs or feet. And her long red hair was loose. It put me in mind of that painting by John Everett Millais."

"*Ophelia*?" I ventured, surprised that the young constable should have some appreciation of art.

"Yes – there was something surreal about the whole affair."

"I see," said Holmes. "And was there anything else that struck you as odd?"

"Only the thin silver chain and charm around her neck. It depicted some sort of mermaid."

I had to express my confusion. "Why did *that* strike you as unusual?"

"Well, six months ago, we had the unpleasant task of removing the dead body of another young woman from the same pond. Around her neck was an identical necklace and charm, and she was dressed in a similar fashion. It was too much of a coincidence."

"Absolutely," echoed Holmes. "So, tell me, when the death of the first woman was investigated, what conclusions were reached?"

The head of the young constable fell, and he looked sheepish. "Sergeant Cotter and I were convinced that it was a case of murder. I spent many hours investigating the death, without success. In the end, the Chief Constable took the difficult decision to shelve the enquiry. The coroner's inquest returned a verdict of *death by misadventure*."

Holmes seemed content to let the matter rest and suggested we make our way to Binsted. The officer obliged and stepped up into the cart. He turned momentarily to ensure that we were both seated safely and then shook the reins of the cart to coax the horse into action.

On the way into the village, we passed Binsted Manor and the impressive park and woodlands surrounding it. The area had been landscaped to resemble some earlier medieval hunting grounds and included a number of tall hybrid oaks, each having its own name and associated folklore – from the Spinning wheel and Staker Oaks, to the Copythorn and

Scotland Oaks. History, mythology, and claims of the supernatural, all helping to shape the identity of this ancient settlement which had Anglo-Saxon roots.

Most of the structures and dwellings in the village spoke of its agricultural heritage; a large flint barn and small land-tied cottages for the labourers working on the bigger farming estates. However, in the midst of this, was a sizeable rectory and the impressive twelfth century church of *St. Mary's*. Farming had clearly brought some prosperity to this quaint rural idyll.

We pulled up briefly at the *Black Horse* inn, which was later to be our resting place for the night. Daubney had already arranged for us to stay for up to four evenings, and we left our travelling bags in the care of the landlady, before heading back out to the cart. For the moment, our destination lay a little further along a track leading from an area known as Goose Green.

The cart came to a stop in the mud beside a rickety wooden gate and stone-built wall, beyond which was a low-lying area of pasture leading to the pond. We stepped down and approached the gate following one of the deep track marks left by an earlier vehicle. I could already see the tall figure of Captain George Drummond talking to a fellow officer who was dressed in a similar fashion to Constable Daubney. I correctly guessed this to be Sergeant Cotter. A large tarpaulin was spread out to their left covering the body of the young girl retrieved from the pond.

With the dog cart secured, we picked our way slowly across the meadow to reach the officers. It was muddy underfoot and criss-crossed with the hoofprints of a substantial number of sheep which were now grouped to our right. Holmes was scanning every inch of the pasture intently as we approached the edge of the pond, so much so that he was initially slow to respond to the outstretched hand and cheery "Hallo!" of the Chief Constable.

"My apologies, Captain Drummond. There is so much to take in. I am keen not to overlook any detail which might prove useful."

The two shook hands and exchanged a few pleasantries before I was reacquainted with Drummond and then introduced to Sergeant Cotter – a solidly built officer with the unmistakable countenance of a one-time pugilist. With the formalities completed, Holmes gestured towards the tarpaulin: "Before we look at the body, I wonder if I might clarify two particular points."

"Certainly," replied Drummond. "I'm sure Sergeant Cotter can assist you."

Holmes looked directly at the sergeant. "Could you point out the precise location where the body was found?"

The officer fairly bellowed out his response: "Just there, sir. Besides the bank on the left. The fabric of her shift was snagged on the low hanging branch of that tree. We got wet feet wading in to disentangle her."

"I see," said Holmes. "That is most helpful. Now, Constable Daubney has already told us that you removed the body earlier this morning. But he didn't mention the name of the dog walker who first discovered the body. It is a detail easily overlooked, but the solitary boot and paw prints running beside the pond from the north testify to the presence of an active man, well over six feet in height, accompanied by an extremely well-trained canine."

Cotter was momentarily speechless, and Captain Drummond shifted uneasily as he, like us, waited for a response. When it came, it felt like a reluctant admission:

"Indeed. That would be Jim Gartner, my brother-in-law. He's an early riser and is always out walking with his black Labrador. He was shocked to see the body and made his way to my house at about five-thirty, rousing me from my bed. I then called on Constable Daubney, who lives but a stone's throw away from my cottage. When he was dressed, we both made our way here."

It was Drummond who now responded: "That's sounds like a convoluted tale, Cotter. You've not mentioned this to me before. Are you quite convinced that your brother-in-law has nothing to do with this affair?"

Cotter was adamant. "Sir, I'd stake my life on it. While he is something of a lovable rogue, he is not a violent or vindictive man. He was ashen when he reached my place. I had no reason to suspect he was involved in any way."

"Well, let us hope that is the case. For the moment I will be guided by Mr. Holmes." He glanced towards my colleague. "How did you deduce so much from a set of footprints?"

Holmes seemed surprised by the polite challenge. "Captain, you have seen me at work before. I merely observe what is before me and make sense of the disparate clues which emerge. While the mud across this pasture has been trampled by many feet, these very distinctive marks are the only ones running north to south. All the others, including those of your men, run from east to west, and back again – the route from the gate. That the man in question is over six feet in height is obvious from the length of the strides he has taken to reach this point. That he was accompanied by a trusted and well-trained dog is equally plain from the closely aligned paw marks beside his own boot prints. The impressions show us that he stopped as soon as he saw the body, most likely tarrying a while to make sense of the vision before him, before then turning and heading off towards the gate and the route into the village. He made no attempt to enter the water."

Drummond was quick to appreciate the significance of this. "Then we can be fairly certain that Gartner played no part in pushing or placing the body in the water?"

"That would appear to be the case. From where he stood, there are no indications of a struggle or anything to suggest that he was carrying or dragging a body. I can see nothing to detract from the testimony he gave to Sergeant Cotter."

"Well, that is some relief. Now, how do you propose to further your investigations, Mr. Holmes?"

My colleague smiled. "With your permission, I would like to spend some time with Dr. Watson and Constable Daubney. Unless you have a particular reason for wanting to stay, could I suggest that we be given free rein to conduct some immediate inquiries? I will of course keep you informed of our progress."

Drummond seemed delighted by the proposed plan of action. "That would be splendid. I have some pressing matters to attend to back at the office. Sergeant Cotter can accompany me in the cart. Beyond that, I will try to ensure that you have all the resources you require in getting to the bottom of this affair. I should also mention that I have arranged with a local surgeon, Dr. Neil Achew, for the body to be transported to the morgue in Arundel sometime around two-thirty. I hope that will be sufficient time for you to glean all that you need to. I imagined that you or Dr. Watson might wish to attend the *post mortem*."

Some moments later we waved the two officers off and turned our attention to the body beneath the tarpaulin. As he stooped to remove the cover, Constable Daubney spoke candidly to Holmes. "Thank you for not revealing all you knew about Sergeant Cotter's brother-in-law. Having worked with you before, I know that you leave a lot of things unsaid."

The detective gave him a knowing grin. "You continue to be very perceptive. I was being euphemistic in describing Jim Gartner as *active* and relaying that he was simply a *dog walker*. In fact, the man is clearly a poacher, who probably rose at first light in the hope of bagging some rabbits or game birds. The two snares which he carelessly and hastily threw into the pond were not difficult to spot in these clear waters. I surmised that when he came across the body and realised the seriousness of what he had discovered, he was desperate not to be caught in possession of such equipment, knowing how that might be viewed by the law. At the same time, his conscience convinced him to report what he had seen to his trusted brother-in-law."

"That is exactly what happened. Sergeant Cotter confided in me. He hoped to protect Jim, knowing that the man's past deeds might well serve to place a noose around his neck if it were determined that this poor girl's death was anything other than an accident or suicide. Jim is well-known in the village and has a genuinely kind heart. He supplies rabbits and pheasants to many in the village who would otherwise have no meat in their diet. If fact, if you dine at the *Black Horse* this evening, there's a fair chance you'll be eating something caught in one of Gartner's snares."

We laughed at this, and I could tell that Holmes had continued to warm to the constable. "Well, I see no necessity for revealing how Jim Gartner makes his living. If he is called to give evidence, he should continue to maintain that he is simply an active dog walker!"

As the corpse was revealed, it was easy to see why Daubney had likened the vision to a painting. The girl was tall and willowy with a mass of long and vibrant red hair. Her skin was almost translucent and her eyes a vivid emerald green. She looked to be no older than seventeen or eighteen years of age, although her waiflike features could easily have belied her years.

I first checked her mouth. The gauntness of her face suggested that she had been malnourished, although her teeth and gums appeared healthy enough. The throat contained no bloody froth or extraneous material which might have suggested death by drowning. The whites of her eyes were clear, showing little sign of any trauma, although I noted that the pupils were heavily dilated. Daubney had been correct in identifying that there were no obvious contusions on the body and both her hands and feet looked clean. The white shift was also remarkably unstained. It suggested that she had been carried to the edge of the pond before being placed carefully into the water. And while toxicology tests would be needed at the *post mortem,* I already felt confident to suggest that the girl had been drugged or poisoned prior to her immersion and that death had not been the result of the hypoxemia and irreversible cerebral anoxia usually associated with submersion in water – a working hypothesis with which Holmes concurred.

"This has been carefully planned," said he. "I see it as significant that there was a full moon last night. We know how much lunacy that can inspire. And the mermaid pendant lends further weight to such a theory. Still, we can be fairly certain that this is where the body entered the water."

I voiced some disquiet. "How can you be certain? You said yourself that there are no visible footprints other than those of the police officers and Jim Gartner. Would we not see the evidence that someone had carried her body up to, or into, the water?"

Holmes smiled enigmatically. "Lying just across the pasture from the gate, this is the easiest point of access to the pond, particularly if you are carrying a body. In terms of the evidence, you have missed a very vital clue. I mentioned earlier that the mud across this field has been trampled by many feet. In doing so, I was not just referring to the human traffic. The sheep have done an excellent job of erasing any footprints we might have seen."

"Are you suggesting that they were put here deliberately, to mask whatever activity took place?"

"It's possible, and certainly a matter we will need to look into." He turned to Daubney. "Who farms this land?"

"Gerald Tilney, one of the wealthiest sheep farmers in the area. His property is less than half a mile away."

"I see. Well, he will no doubt be expecting us to speak to him as the body has been found on his land and word of the death is likely to have circulated now to all parts of the village. In many respects, it seems odd that he hasn't already put in an appearance."

We were bathed in bright sunlight and the temperature had begun to rise steadily. Holmes removed his Inverness cape and placed it on a corner of the tarpaulin, before moving in with his magnifying glass to take a closer look at the girl's neck. With an expression of intense interest, he was drawn to the silver chain and pendant. "This has no hallmark, so it's not a professional job. That said, it's exquisitely made and hardly the work of an amateur either. Most likely a special commission, as we already know that more than one was made."

There was little more to be determined from the body at that point. Holmes agreed that it would be crucial for me to attend the *post mortem* and to collaborate with the surgeon sent to collect the cadaver.

Our attention then switched to the death of the first girl. Holmes asked Daubney to explain what he had discovered in the earlier investigation. Daubney turned to his little black pocketbook, where he had clearly kept copious notes. Holmes looked suitably impressed.

"One night in September last year, I received a visit from our vicar, Stephen Dutton. He said he'd been unable to sleep and had taken a walk around the village to clear his head. His route took him close to Goose Green and this pond, which everyone refers to as the *Knucker Hole*. It was close to ten o'clock, on a bright, moonlit night – another full moon in fact – and as Dutton paused to look across the pond, he saw the body of a young woman in the water. She was lying on her back and not moving. He believed her to be dead.

"I followed Dutton back to the pond and saw for myself that he was not mistaken. In amongst the reeds, I could see the girl, and with a series of ligger boards I managed to pull her body from the water. I should say at this point, that over the years the pond has been the scene of half a dozen drownings and suicides. Many of the superstitious locals believe it to be a bottomless pit which contains a water-dwelling monster called a '*knucker*.' As a result, few people are brave enough to venture near it at night and recently there has been a lot more talk about the so-called 'water spirits.'

"The young woman was dressed in a white shift identical to the one we're looking at now. She was also slender, with long hair and elfin-like features, and around her neck was a mermaid pendant. There was nothing to explain her death, and I initially assumed it to be another case of suicide. Dr.

Achew came to view the body and quickly concluded the same, saying that a *post mortem* was not warranted."

I expressed some surprise. "Really? That seems a little odd. I'll be sure to quiz him about that later."

Daubney continued: "Through my subsequent inquiries, I discovered that the girl, whose name was Jenny Matthews, was fifteen years of age and had been employed only weeks before as a maid at one of the larger dairy farms in the area. Prior to that, she had been an orphan at the local workhouse, where she had resided for two years.

"It seemed strange to me, but the incident attracted little attention in the village. Even her employer, farmer and widower Tom Boyne, appeared non-plussed when told about her passing. I began to reflect more on the circumstances surrounding the death. If Matthews had taken her own life by walking into the water to drown, how were her bare feet so clean? And did she not struggle in those final moments? I could not conceive of someone lying in such a serene fashion after drowning.

"The mermaid pendant was the same as the one on this girl. When I spoke to the master at the workhouse, he said that no girl there would ever be in possession of such an expensive item and suggested that she must have acquired it after gaining employment. Yet, Boyne could not recollect seeing Matthews with such a necklace. I did visit the two jewellers based in Arundel, both of whom said they did not recognise the pendant, although one mentioned that there was a craft worker locally who fashioned trinkets out of silver. Unfortunately, I had no opportunity to speak to her given the events which followed.

"I felt the death to be suspicious and told Captain Drummond about my concerns. He was not convinced and told me to bring the case to a close, to enable the coroner's inquest to be concluded. Jenny Matthews was buried a few days later in the churchyard of *St. Mary's* in a ceremony conducted by Stephen Dutton. I felt it my duty to be there, imagining that the burial of a former workhouse girl would not be well-attended. However, on the day, I was a little surprised to see that in addition to the vicar and four pallbearers – who carried her rather ornate coffin – there were eight people at the funeral. Some I might have expected, such as Tom Boyne and two young women from the workhouse who had known her. But there were others from across the village: Dr. Neil Achew; Gerald Tilney; Arthur Brimham, the blacksmith; Felicity King, a dressmaker; and Tristan Tarnhow-Miller, our resident historian.

Holmes gave this information some considerable thought. "It's a little surprising that a former workhouse girl should be given such a funeral, particularly in the case of an alleged suicide. Most clergymen would insist on a pauper's burial outside the churchyard. And the fact that she was buried in a decent coffin suggests that someone intervened to pay the funeral expenses."

"My thoughts exactly, Mr. Holmes. I wondered if one of those present knew something of the girl's demise, for church services at *St Mary's* are poorly attended more often than not. After the funeral, I spoke to the vicar and asked about the ceremony. He explained that the church maintained a contingency fund for such situations. He had refused to sanction an interment outside the churchyard for he felt that everyone was entitled to a decent Christian burial. The attendees were part of a newly established church group which supported this ethos.

"Had I not been instructed by the Chief Constable to desist from any further inquiries, I would have interviewed all of the funeral attendees. Now, with the discovery of this second body, it might be useful to do just that."

"I couldn't agree more," replied Holmes. "Now, was there anything else?"

"Yes, just one other point. When we arrived at the gate this morning, I noticed that there were distinct wheel marks in the mud from what looked to be a single vehicle. I have recorded the width of these in my pocketbook. The information may yet prove useful."

"Excellent, well-spotted! I had noted the same myself. You have the makings of an excellent detective!"

Daubney blushed but beamed in response.

"A pattern seems to be emerging," observed Holmes. "It appears that these girls have been chosen very deliberately. I am confident that we were looking at a series of carefully planned, possibly even ritualistic, murders. That is the only reasonable explanation for not one, but two girls, who have been found lying dead in a posed condition. Not to mention that both were similarly dressed and wearing an identical silver pendant.

"Do you know if there were any similar cases prior to the death of the first girl?"

"Not that I could find. The earlier drownings and suicides I referred to did not seem to fit the pattern of these deaths."

"Splendid. You have given us some valuable leads to pursue. I suggest we start with Jim Gartner, the poacher, and the vicar, before then speaking to all those you observed at the funeral. That should keep us busy for a couple of days. Watson, would you be kind enough to stay with the body until the surgeon arrives and sit in on the *post mortem*? I can then meet you a little later back at the *Black Horse*."

I was pleased to oblige on both counts. They set off shortly afterwards and I had ten minutes to wait until the surgeon arrived on a small tumbril cart in the company of a strapping lad who had been brought along to assist. I greeted them warmly and hastily explained to Dr. Achew that I'd already had a chance to examine the body. From the off, the fellow proved to be pompous and disagreeable, saying in his plummy voice that it was highly irregular for another doctor to interfere when he was responsible for conducting local autopsies. I made it clear that Captain Drummond had already authorised my attendance, but this did little to placate the man, who then stormed off across the pasture saying I could conduct the *post mortem* myself! With the body placed safely in the cart, I had little choice but to do just that and accompany the assistant back to the morgue.

Supporting my earlier hypothesis, I found nothing in the examination to indicate that the death had been the result of drowning. But my toxicology tests identified significant traces of ethanol, morphine, and meconic acid, suggesting that she had died from a lethal dose of laudanum. Unfortunately, because of the immersion in water and the time that had elapsed, I was not able to determine with any accuracy the likely time of death.

There was no evidence to show that the girl had been assaulted in any way. However, the most significant new information revealed by the examination was the fact that the young woman was in the early stages of pregnancy, a factor which I felt sure would have some bearing on the case.

I began to scrub up and clear away all the autopsy equipment with the help of the mortuary assistant. I then wrote up what I had done and the conclusions I had reached in the medical records which Dr. Achew maintained. Doing so, I looked back on some of the surgeon's own notes. Finding an entry for the earlier death of Jenny Matthews, I was able to confirm what Daubney had told us – for Achew had indeed recorded that suicide was the cause of death and no *post mortem* was required. I reflected on this and the man's extraordinary behaviour that afternoon. *Was he implicated in some way and trying to cover up the deaths, I wondered?* It was certainly something to share with Holmes.

By the time I left the mortuary, it was almost five o'clock, and I set off to walk the two miles from Arundel back to the village of Binsted. When I reached the *Black Horse,* I was greeted warmly by the landlady who said our bags had been taken up to our rooms, and an evening meal would be served in the tap room from seven o'clock. It came as no surprise to learn that rabbit was on the menu!

****

In the company of PC Daubney, we sat down for our evening meal at a quarter past seven. The meat was delicious and served with generous helpings of roasted potatoes, parsnips, and carrots, covered by a thick onion gravy. Holmes said that he and Daubney had made good progress that afternoon, but invited me first to explain what I had discovered during the *post mortem.*

Both were astonished to hear how Dr. Achew had reacted in leaving me to complete the examination. I expressed my concerns, saying that he might be implicated, and pointing out that as a surgeon he would have ready access to laudanum, the drug that had killed the latest victim. Holmes postulated that if the doctor had been trying to cover up the nature of the death, it seemed odd that he then let me conduct the *post mortem.* That said, he agreed that we needed to keep an open mind about the surgeon.

He was not surprised to hear that I was unable to determine an accurate window for the time of death. In response, he said it was unlikely that the body had been placed in the pond prior to the previous evening. Had that occurred, he felt certain that it would have been discovered by one of the many locals who seemed to gravitate towards the pond during the daytime. Daubney had already confirmed that it was a popular route for farm workers and the like during daylight hours, although few were brave enough to approach the *Knucker Hole* after dark.

The revelation that the young woman had been pregnant seemed to shock Daubney, who then speculated that there might also have been a sexual element to Jenny Matthew's death. Holmes concurred, saying that it certainly couldn't be ruled out at this stage. He then went on to explain what the two of them had discovered that afternoon.

"Our first visit was to Jim Gartner, the poacher. He described how he had been out after midnight hoping to snare some rabbits. The conditions had been perfect – a full moon and a cloudless sky – and as dawn was fast approaching his bag was full, so he and the Labrador were heading for home. But close to the pond, he heard some whistling and commands being shouted to another dog which was driving a flock of sheep down from the hills to the lower pasture in which the *Knucker Hole* sits. He only just avoided being seen by the shepherd, whom he recognised to be Gerald Tilney. He thought it curious that the man should be moving his livestock in the early hours of the morning. Shortly afterwards, when he was sure that Tilney had gone, he continued onwards towards the pond, where he then saw the body."

My colleague had next visited the rectory, while PC Daubney had sought to track down the craft worker he had been told about by the jeweller in Arundel.

"Stephen Dutton is a curious fellow," said Holmes, draining what remained of his mug of stout. "A timid, small-chested man whose Lancashire accent belies his status as the *local* vicar. In fact, he has only been at his ministry for a year and has yet to be accepted by many of the villagers. He described them as 'virtually pagan' and said that superstition is rife, with ghostly tales and supernatural sightings being talked about frequently. Much of the attention appears to be focused on the *Knucker Hole* – which is believed to contain a water-dwelling monster which lures the unsuspecting to their doom! He said it didn't help that some recently uncovered church records had given credence to the myths surrounding this Old English *Nicor*, which Dutton had been told was first mentioned in the epic poem *Beowulf*."

I chuckled at this and then asked: "Did he say anything further about the discovery of Jenny Matthews's body?"

"No, his account tallied with that of young Daubney here. But he did say more about the burial. When pressed, he admitted that the donations into the church contingency fund had come from the newly established church group, all of whom had proved to be most benevolent."

He rose at that point to get each of us another pint and invited Daubney to share with me what he had discovered. The constable had apparently walked to nearby Walberton where he eventually found the craft worker. Sarah Fowler had a small workshop set within some woods where she produced a range of silver trinkets. When shown one of the mermaid pendants, she confirmed with pride that it was indeed one of hers. Daubney had been careful not to reveal the nature of his enquiries and asked if she could recall who had commissioned the piece. Fowler said that it had been nine or ten months since the man had first placed the order for six of the mermaid charms. He had not left his name, but had paid for the jewellery in advance, collecting them, as agreed, a month later. Asked to describe the man, she recollected only that he was an older gentleman with greying hair, who was extremely well spoken and 'definitely not a local.'

Having agreed to meet back in the village, Holmes and Daubney's final call had been to the sheep farmer, Gerald Tilney. Holmes described him as "a gruff, unprepossessing man, in his late-fifties, who lives alone."

He talked me through the encounter: "He refused to let us in and stood in the doorway of the farmhouse in a very territorial manner. He said he knew nothing of the girl whose body had been discovered. I asked if he had seen anyone on his land or close to the pond the previous night. 'No,' came the reply. 'In any case, Tom Boyne and Arthur Brimham were here that night for a few hands of poker. I didn't venture outside. When they left just before midnight I went straight to bed.'

"PC Daubney then asked casually: 'What time did you get up this morning?' Tilney looked at him with some intensity, as if trying to ascertain what Daubney was driving at. When he answered, he was non-specific. 'I rose early – I had a few jobs to deal with on the farm.' Daubney then said, 'Yes, I understand you were out in the early hours moving your sheep. I'm surprised you didn't see the body yourself being so close to the pond.' This clearly rattled the man, although he maintained that his focus had been on the task at hand and the importance of getting the sheep down from the hills for shearing later that week. He added that when he had secured the northern gate to the meadow, he had not gone near the pond. It was a telling response, Watson, for it proves that

Tilney was lying and most likely involved in the girl's murder."

I was not sure I followed. "Well, it certainly confirms he moved the sheep. But how was he lying?"

"Our working hypothesis was that someone had moved the sheep down from the hills to cover up the footprints near the pond. In admitting to the act, Tilney claimed the animals were being moved in readiness for shearing. That was a lie. Growing up in the Yorkshire Dales, I know that hill sheep live and lamb in the uplands for much of the year. It is only in May or early summer that they are driven down to lowland pastures for the purposes of shearing."

"Then we have a significant suspect," I replied excitedly.

Holmes grinned widely. "Constable Daubney and I certainly believe so, although I'm sure there is much more to uncover. I suggest we resume our investigations first thing tomorrow and see where they lead us."

****

It was shortly after eight o'clock the following morning when PC Daubney met us once more at the *Black Horse*. With our breakfast completed we set off on foot towards the northern end of the village where Tom Boyne's dairy farm was located.

The man proved to be much more amenable than Tilney. He welcomed us in, offering tea as soon as we were seated in his spacious kitchen. He said he knew nothing of the poor girl who had died and queried why we were asking questions about "another suicide." Daubney said that the Chief Constable wanted a thorough investigation to ensure that the circumstances of the death were fully explored.

Holmes then asked him if he had seen anyone near the pond when he was over at Tilney's playing cards. He appeared to smirk at this, before saying that he could not recollect seeing anyone on the walk over from the village. When he left at the end of the evening he was in the company of Arthur Brimham. Again, he saw no one. When then quizzed about the death and funeral of Jenny Matthews, his former maid, Boyne admitted that she had been "a dependable employee" and he had felt it his duty "to see that she had a good send-off." He added little beyond this.

Our next call was to Arthur Brimham himself, whose forge was only a short walk from the dairy farm. In his early forties, the bachelor was something of a brute, with an upper body well-suited to the bending and shaping of iron. In his strong local accent, he said he could only spare a few minutes of his time, as he was rushing to fulfil an order which had to be completed that day. He claimed to know nothing of the deceased girl and confirmed that he had gone over to Gerald Tilney's at about seven o'clock that night to play cards. The only person he saw on the journey over to the farm was Felicity King, the dressmaker. When asked if he had known Jenny Matthews, Brimham replied in the negative. But when then challenged as to why he had attended the funeral of someone he did not know, the man's composure seemed less convincing. All he could say in response was, "I've recently joined the local church group and thought I ought to attend."

Holmes was keen to cover as much ground as we could that day, and suggested that we next visit the local workhouse, which was situated midway between Binsted and Arundel. It was a large industrial building in which the inmates were required to work in a variety of trades depending on their age and gender. The master in charge was Silas Carstairs, a gruff, heavily bearded man, with a commanding manner. His upstairs office overlooked an area in which a large number of looms were being operated by the women and girls of the workhouse.

PC Daubney explained the nature of our inquiries and asked if any of the girls were missing from the workhouse. Carstairs confirmed that a seventeen-year-old, by the name of Kathleen Tomkinson, had absconded two days earlier. It had not been the first time she had run away, and he referred to her as "a disturbed and troublesome girl." He agreed to send someone over to the morgue to check if the deceased was Tomkinson.

We then talked about the earlier death. Carstairs had a slightly better opinion of Jenny Matthews, whom he described as "a popular and diligent girl." Holmes asked him how she had come to secure the job on Tom Boyne's farm. He said it was not uncommon for former workhouse girls to be taken on by local farmers.

Daubney had the names of the two girls he had seen at the funeral. He asked if we could speak to them, and they were brought to us by a sour-faced matron. When we insisted that the interview take place in private, it was with some reluctance that the master withdrew from his office. The girls said they had been friendly with Matthews, describing her as a pretty girl who always attracted the attentions of men who brought deliveries to the workhouse.

As we were leaving the office, I was struck by two items sitting on the master's large oak desk. The first was a package containing a bundle of clothing which had been opened sufficiently to reveal its contents. Inside were a dozen white shifts. In another corner, atop a large stack of paperwork, was an invoice for thirty new shovels – the letterhead showing that they had been supplied by the local blacksmith. I felt certain that my colleagues had noted the same.

Outside, on the walk back into Binsted, the three of us reflected on the new information. "The master's disclosures sounded like a fictional melodrama," I ventured, "with all that talk about a runaway girl who was *disturbed and troublesome* and another who was *pretty* and *attracting the attentions of men*. It sounds as if there were clearly some sexual element to all of this. I wonder if the first victim might also have been pregnant when killed?"

"Quite possibly," replied Holmes. "We may yet find out. If the need arises, the Chief Constable may be able to seek permission to have the body exhumed. These are dark waters, gentlemen. Hearing that it was *not uncommon for former workhouse girls to be taken on by local farmers*, I believe we can begin to see how widower, Tom Boyne, and the lonesome Gerald Tilney might be implicated."

"Yes," agreed Daubney, "and their bachelor friend, Arthur Brimham. I think we all noted his invoice on the master's desk. If he has been making deliveries to the workhouse, it's conceivable that he may have developed some rapport with both Kathleen Tomkinson and Jenny Matthews."

"Indeed. And an order for thirty shovels would require a vehicle. When we visited him earlier, I noted that Brimham has a small cart. I wonder if the dimensions of the wheels match those you found in the mud near the *Knucker Hole*? If they do, Brimham becomes another strong suspect, with the means to move both people and bodies about without attracting too much attention."

"I'll make it my mission to find out, Mr. Holmes! I will probably need to tread carefully but should be able to complete that task discreetly sometime this evening."

"Excellent! And what do we make of the bundle of white shifts that were also on the master's desk?" Holmes's observational skills had never been in doubt.

"It suggests that the dressmaker, Felicity King, may also be part of this growing conspiracy," said I. "She is yet another member of the new church group."

"True enough. And it may be as well to visit her next."

Felicity King was a slim, fair-haired woman in her early-fifties. She looked to have a thriving business which she ran from a large cottage near Strawberry Fair Fields. In the previous year, she had taken on two young seamstresses to keep up with the demand for her clothing, which she said was mainly working clothes for local mill workers. When asked if this included any items for the workhouse, she responded without hesitation, saying that she received regular orders for cotton shifts which many of the woman and girls wore as underwear. Asked about the funeral of Jenny Matthews, she confirmed that she had not known the girl, but her strong Christian faith had compelled her to "show some compassion at the demise of such an innocent soul."

Having left the cottage, Daubney was of the view that the dressmaker had been telling the truth. I was inclined to agree with him. Holmes said he had yet to form a view and asked the constable to direct us towards the surgery of Dr. Achew. He explained that we would speak to the surgeon and then stop for some lunch at the *Black Horse*. After no more than four or five minutes we arrived at an attractive thatched cottage standing on its own beside a small beck. When Dr. Achew responded to the doorbell, Daubney explained that the three of us had a few questions about the two girls who had died in the pond.

The surgeon displayed none of his earlier tetchiness and said that he was only too willing to assist. Seated inside his small, but well-furnished, parlour – which clearly doubled as his consulting room – Achew voiced an immediate and heartfelt confession: "Dr. Watson, I must apologise for my conduct yesterday. It was unwarranted and highly unprofessional. I wrongly believed that this second death was, like the first, a simple case of suicide. As such, I was at a loss to understand why a second doctor should be asked to assist. Having spoken to the Chief Constable today, I realise now that there are some concerns about both deaths. I have read your excellent autopsy report and appreciate that I was too hasty in my judgment. I will also be frank in admitting that I should have conducted a *post mortem* on the body of Jenny Matthews. I work hard to meet all the demands on my time as a local doctor and have struggled to keep up with the additional burden of my role at the mortuary. I was merely trying to save time on what I thought was an obvious case of *felo de se*."

The turnaround was most unexpected, and I thanked him for the apology. Holmes then asked him tactfully about the cause of death and the use of laudanum. "Have you come across any other cases locally where a tincture of opium has been instrumental in someone's death?"

"No, Mr. Holmes. That's a first as far as I can recollect. It's not an obvious way to despatch someone. I keep a small quantity of laudanum in a locked cabinet at the back of the cottage. I checked this morning and can confirm that the cabinet has not been tampered with and none of my supply is missing."

We had little option but to take him at his word. PC Daubney then asked, rather obliquely, if the doctor had commissioned any jewellery in the past year. Dr. Achew responded in any equally obscure fashion, seemingly unfazed by the line of inquiry. "Ah, I see that my private life has been the subject of some gossip. I have not, Constable, but may be in the market for a ring sometime soon!"

There was no follow up to this, for none of us knew quite how to respond. As a final question, Holmes enquired about where the doctor obtained his supply of surgical drugs. "There is only one chemist locally," he replied, "Mr. Stevens in Arundel." With this, our brief visit was at an end. We emerged from the cottage to find that the temperature had dropped and a light drizzle had begun to fall. Fortunately, it was but a short stroll to the inn where a warm meal awaited us.

Over a lunch of baked potatoes and stewed beef, we reflected on Dr. Achew's curious manner. Holmes was inclined to believe the surgeon's tale about being busy and saving himself the additional workload of conducting a *post mortem*. "He is certainly very pompous but seemed genuine enough in responding to the question about jewellery, although I'm at a loss to know why he then mentioned the ring!"

Daubney agreed but reminded us that the description Sarah Fowler had given him of the man ordering the pendants did sound very much like the doctor. We had to concede that his point was well made.

With our lunch completed, we left the inn and walked back to Goose Green. Our destination was the *Old Manse* lived in by Tristan Tarnhow-Miller. As we approached the door, I could hear a violin playing the first part of Richard Wagner's opera cycle *Der Ring des Nibelungen*, a piece which Holmes himself was fond of performing. Tarnhow-Miller was convivial and having dispensed with his violin was quick to offer us tea and a slice of madeira cake. He explained that he was originally from St Albans, and, having graduated from Cambridge University, had taken a job as an archivist at the British Museum. Now retired, he had settled in the village a year earlier and had become something of a local historian, uncovering long-lost information about the village which he enjoyed sharing with his neighbours.

The man's library demonstrated the broad range of his interests, from academic texts on philosophy and religion, to historical novels and poetry. But it was two books which sat in pride of place, and alone, on an ornate sideboard that seemed to catch Holmes's eye. The first was a volume of poetry by Sebastian Evans, entitled *Brother Fabian's Manuscript*, while the second was a newly published work by Andrew Lang, entitled *The Yellow Fairy Book*. My colleague observed casually that the first volume looked to be a fascinating book, to which the former archivist replied: "Yes, one of my favourites, signed for me by the poet himself. We were undergraduates together."

When asked about the two deaths, the man said they were terrible affairs. He had not met either of the girls in his short time living in Binsted. He had tried to immerse himself in all aspects of village life, including the setting up of a new church group to counter the pervasive influence of the pagan folklore which many of the locals espoused. It was he who had encouraged the group to contribute to the contingency fund which was used to pay for Jenny Matthews's funeral.

We left Tarnhow-Miller after half an hour, with Holmes saying that he had been most helpful. I was not so sure that the visit had elicited any useful information, but kept the thought to myself. As we crossed Goose Green, the great detective said that many features of the case were beginning to fall into place. He then announced that we would need to head back into Arundel to complete three tasks. Daubney was to visit Mr. Stephens, the chemist, to enquire about recent purchases of laudanum. Holmes planned to stop off at the police station to brief Captain Drummond on all that we had discovered. And I was tasked with the most bewildering assignment of the three – to locate the town's library and see if I could track down copies of the two books we had seen in Tarnhow-Miller's study. Holmes provided no further explanation!

The light drizzle had now given way to some sporadic bursts of sunshine which made the walk into town a little more tolerable. We had already covered a fair distance on our travels that day and I could feel the first twinges of stiffness in my leg. Fortuitously for me, the library was situated on the outskirts of Binsted. I left Holmes and Daubney at that point, agreeing to meet up with them later back at the inn.

The reading room of the small library proved to be quiet and cosy. I approached one of the young librarians and enquired about the two books. She explained that the Andrew Lang book had only been released the previous year and the first print run had sold out very quickly. As a result, the library still had the volume on order. However, it did have a copy of the Sebastian Evans volume and I was directed towards a shelf on which sat *Brother Fabian's Manuscript*.

I seated myself close to the wood burner in the reading room and began to flick through the pages. It took me a while to find any poem which might have some relevance to our inquiries, but finally came across one containing the following verse:

Whereby the marshes boometh the bittern,

Neckar the soulless one sits with his ghittern.

Sits inconsolable, friendless and foeless.

Waiting his destiny, – Neckar the soulless.

The word *Neckar* sounded very much like the words *Knucker* and *Nicor* which we had already been told about. I copied the verse in my notebook and thanked the librarian for her assistance. Having been warmed through, the journey back to the *Black Horse* did not seem too onerous.

That evening, we reconvened in the tap room. Holmes said Captain Drummond was pleased to learn that the investigation was progressing well. Constable Daubney talked us through his visit to the chemist's. Unsurprisingly, Mr. Stevens said that most of the regular purchasers of laudanum were doctors and veterinary surgeons and – with reference to the *poisons book*, which he was required to keep – confirmed that Dr. Achew was one of these. But he also recollected, that in the August of the previous year, he had supplied a red bottle of the tincture to a man he had not seen before. He could not recall what the customer looked like but remembered glancing at the book and thinking that his name was unusual – for he had signed it *Mr. Death*. While he knew this to be a well-established British surname, which is pronounced 'dee-ath', he found it rather curious.

Holmes responded with a dry chuckle. He then invited me to share what I had uncovered at the library. I explained that I was only able to track down the Sebastian Evans book and had found just one poem which seemed to resonate with our inquiry. When I read out the piece, Holmes was effusive in his praise: "Well done, Watson! I knew I recollected something of the book when I saw it in the study. The poetry collection was required reading when I was at boarding school, although I have to say I found its contents terribly dull!"

I was a little baffled, as was Daubney. "Does this have any particular significance, Mr. Holmes?" he asked, with a look of some consternation.

"Absolutely! What are we to make of this Tristan Tarnhow-Miller? The supposedly upright newcomer who has been instrumental in setting up the church group with its contingency fund. He said he was trying to *counter the pervasive influence of the pagan folklore* being spread in the village, and yet it seems he might be the very source of that gossip as the self-appointed *local historian*. When we arrived at the house, he was playing part of Wagner's ring cycle – a story featuring female river mermaids known as the *Nixe*. And now we learn that his favourite book contains a verse about a creature called the *Neckar*. I also have little doubt that it was Tarnhow-Miller who recently uncovered the church records referring to the Old English *Nicor* – a discovery which he was only too keen to share with the vicar."

"Well, he's certainly immersed himself in all aspects of village life," I added, before coming to the crux of the matter: "Do you think he set up the church group to cover his more sinister activities, and then began to circulate the stories about water spirits to keep people away from the *Knucker Hole*?"

"That is my contention, but I need more evidence to make a compelling case against the man. For the moment, we must carry on with our inquiries."

****

As he had done the previous day, Daubney met us for breakfast. The smile on his face suggested that he had some good news. He went on to say that he had been busy overnight on a covert task. Using the dimensions of the wheel tracks he had noted earlier, he set out under cover of darkness to identify how many people in the village owned a vehicle with wheels to match. There were only three – a carriage owned by Dr. Achew, the dog cart used by Arthur Brimham, and a trap in the possession of a local butcher. He discounted the latter as it was found to have a broken axle and had clearly sat in an outbuilding for some time.

Holmes was delighted, for this clearly placed one of our suspects at the pond around the likely time of the death. The question now was whether that man was Arthur Brimham or Dr. Achew.

I too had some news to share. A brief note had been delivered to the inn that morning by the young mortuary assistant. In it, he said that the matron from the workhouse had visited the morgue the previous evening to identify the body. She had confirmed that it was that of Kathleen Tomkinson. And while surprised to learn that the girl had been pregnant, she said it was not the first time that one of their girls had absconded and fallen prey to the lecherous men of the village.

Once again, Holmes was elated. "Capital! It seems our endeavours have begun to pay off. Now, we have one important task to complete first thing today. It was something that was nagging away at me after our visit to Felicity King yesterday. I had quite forgotten about it until I began to brief the Chief Constable. Do you remember what Arthur Brimham said when I asked him to confirm whether he had gone to Gerald Tilney's to play cards?"

I had to be honest in saying that I could not recall what was said. Yet Daubney once again came to the rescue. Pulling his pocketbook from inside his tunic, he flicked through the pages and found the relevant notes: "He said he was at Tilney's, but added something else. On the journey over to the farm at about seven o'clock he had apparently seen someone else – namely, Felicity King, the dressmaker."

"Bravo!" said Holmes. "We need to ask her why she was out walking at that time."

Felicity King seemed a little surprised to see the three of us on her doorstep for a second time. Nevertheless, she was cordial and invited us into her sumptuous parlour. Declining the offer of refreshments, Holmes indicated that we would not need more than a few minutes of her time. He said he understood she had been out walking in the village around seven o'clock on the evening before the body was found. "Did you see anyone else on your travels?" he then asked.

The dressmaker blushed and her composure changed rapidly. Struggling to look Holmes in the eye, she responded by saying that she could not recollect seeing anyone on the walk, but had not, in any case, ventured far. She asked if she could rely on us to be discreet with any information which she then shared. Holmes gave her that assurance, and she went on to explain: "I was visiting the home of Dr. Achew. In recent months, the two of us have become very close friends. In fact, we spent the evening together, and Neil walked me home shortly before midnight. You may understand why I would not like that fact to be made public. In a small village like this, my reputation and business could be severely affected by such an admission."

Holmes smiled and said that he understood completely, before rephrasing his original question: "Do you mind me asking if you saw or heard anyone while walking back with Dr. Achew?"

She took a few moments to answer, for the query had clearly jogged something in her memory. When she did respond, the disclosure was most enlightening. "I did not *see* anyone but remember now that I *heard* something. And it was the same on the walk over to Neil's. I was aware of a vehicle passing on the other side of the green close to the beck. I did not see who it was but did wonder why someone was travelling at night. And as I was saying goodbye to Neil on my doorstep, heard a similar noise someway off in the distance."

Holmes thanked her for her time and said that she had been most helpful. He assured her once again that the personal information she had disclosed would be treated as confidential.

Outside on the track leading from Strawberry Fair Fields, Holmes talked in hushed tones about the significance of what she had revealed. "I have no reason to believe that Miss King is lying. She clearly has an alibi for where she was that evening, and, in admitting to her dalliance with Dr. Achew, has provided him with one too. It also helps to explain Dr. Achew's bizarre reference to a *ring*. He clearly has plans to propose to her and believed that we knew about his romance! On a more serious note, we now have more convincing evidence that Arthur Brimham's cart was used that night."

"Yes," said Daubney, excitedly. "If Dr. Achew was not involved, it means that the wheel marks we saw near the gate were from the blacksmith's cart. Miss King may not have seen *him*, but Brimham clearly saw her on the journey over to Tilney's."

"Agreed. And he wasn't on foot – something he could not, of course, share with us."

Our conversation was halted by the sound of somebody running towards us. Up ahead we could see Jim Gartner, the poacher, in full flight, his hob-nail boots clattering on the stone cobbles beneath his feet and his faithful Labrador running closely beside him. As he reached us, he stopped, and having taken some seconds to catch his breath, said we should follow him. "I've seen something near the pond, Mr. Holmes. Something which might be significant. I heard that you were in the village and got to you as soon as I could."

We headed off quickly in the direction of the *Knucker Hole*. Gartner continued to share snippets of information in short, breathless bursts, as he led the way. He had been out poaching once again and had seen something glistening in one of the bushes to the south of the pond. Reaching the spot, he saw concealed within the dense undergrowth a large hessian sack into which had been thrust some colourful looking garments. It was the metallic braiding along the collar of one of these which had drawn his eye.

Having climbed the gate at the end of the track, we made our way across the meadow towards the oval-shaped *Knucker Hole*, with the sheep scattering before us. Gartner went to the left, skirting around a thicket of trees and bushes, before then stopping at a point he had marked with a neckerchief.

Holmes picked his way through the bushes, scanning the ground carefully as he did so. When he emerged he was holding the hessian sack. Daubney said it had not been there when he and Sergeant Cotter first searched the area. Holmes concurred, adding, "There are some fairly indistinct footprints, which were definitely not here two days ago."

I gazed with fascination at the emerging contents. Holmes withdrew four highly decorated robes – in red, gold, and black – which looked to be gowns of a ceremonial or religious nature. In the sack below them were four matching hoods with eye holes. He scrutinised each item thoroughly, saying initially that there was nothing to indicate where the garments had come from. And then, having singled out one of the robes which had significantly more braiding and decoration than the others, he exclaimed: "We have him, gentlemen! At the bottom of this exceptionally tailored fabric is a tiny label sewn into the velvet lining. It reads simply: *Emmanuel College*. We have him!"

"Who, Holmes?" I asked in confusion.

"Why, Tarnhow-Miller of course. He graduated from Cambridge University and told us he was a contemporary of the poet Sebastian Evans. Evans was a student at *Emmanuel College* as my former house master was fond of reminding us every time we studied the poetry book!"

With the robes stored safely back in the hessian sack, we trooped back to the *Black Horse* for a well-earned pint of local ale. Holmes made a particular point of thanking Jim Gartner for his assistance and when the poacher had left us we discussed what to do next.

"I believe we have enough evidence to obtain arrest warrants for all of our suspects," began Holmes. "The deaths of Kathleen Tomkinson and Jenny Matthews came at the hands of four manipulative and malevolent men led by the Tristan Tarnhow-Miller. I believe he commissioned the mermaid pendants and also obtained the laudanum which was used to despatch Kathleen Tomkinson. Only he would be brazen enough to sign himself off as *Mr. Death* and he is the only one of the four who does not have a local accent. And while there are many more details to be uncovered, I am keen for us to act quickly in detaining Tarnhow-Miller, Tilney, Boyne and Brimham."

PC Daubney was in complete agreement. "I know that Captain Drummond will support such a plan. The case against the men is compelling and if we don't stop them now there is every likelihood that further young women will die at their hands."

****

With the required arrest warrants secured that evening, plans were made for a detachment of officers from Arundel police station to detain all four men at dawn the following day. Captain Drummond authorised PC Daubney to lead the operation. When Holmes and I arrived at the station at nine o'clock that morning, we were told that everything had gone smoothly and the four men were being housed in separate cells.

Daubney's decision to keep the men isolated until each had been interrogated in turn, proved to be decisive in uncovering all the facts behind the crimes they had committed. He was convinced that Tarnhow-Miller would say nothing to implicate himself, so interviewed the others before speaking to him. The three local men proved to be weak-willed when presented with the case against them, with each seeking to play down his role in the affair while providing crucial testimony against the others. By the end of the day, the full horror of the case had been laid bare.

For some years, Arthur Brimham had been coercing girls from the workhouse for his own immoral pleasures. His friends, Tilney and Boyne, had asked to be involved, with the girls then being taken to one of the two farms in Brimham's cart. Afterwards, they were returned to the workhouse. However, in the case of Jenny Matthews, Boyne went one step further and arranged to employ the girl to keep her within his grasp. Tristan Tarnhow-Miller then moved into the village. Learning of their activities, he persuaded them to add a little more theatricality to their seedy pursuits.

The former archivist was charismatic, and something of a misogynist, establishing a new church group to mask his more sinister plans. Through his friendship with the poet Sebastian Evans, Tarnhow-Miller had been introduced to the legend of the *Neckar*, a subject on which he would become fixated as the years rolled by. Using the archives of the British Museum, he had access to numerous documents which set out the mythology of the shapeshifting water spirits commonly found in Germanic and Scandinavian folklore and variously named as *neck, nicor, nixie* or *nokken*. One spirit form lured people into rivers and ponds, like Wagner's mermaids. A second group was the water-dwelling creatures which brought prosperity to those who appeased them. To reap the benefits of their benevolence, Tarnhow-Miller believed that human sacrifices were required. He drew on a poem written by Andrew Lang called *The Nixie of the Mill-Pond*, which featured in *The Yellow Fairy Book* which we had seen in the study of the *Old Manse*. In this, an evil water spirit makes a deal with a miller to restore his wealth in exchange for the sacrifice of his son.

Tarnhow-Miller told the others about the power of the water spirits, their need to be assuaged, and the personal benefits that this would generate. He provided them with some ceremonial robes from his university days and named the group *The Neckar*. Under the light of each full moon, they would meet at the sacred *Knucker Hole* in an attempt to instigate a reawakening of the water spirits.

It did not take long for the group to be persuaded that a first sacrifice was required when Jenny Matthews announced she was pregnant. They believed that her disappearance would not attract too much attention. Tarnhow-Miller purchased a bottle of laudanum and gave it to Boyne, who used it to kill the girl. They then transported her body to the pond in Brimham's cart, where she was ceremonially placed in the water wearing one of the mermaid pendants. Kathleen Tomkinson was despatched in the same way at Tilney's farm with the cart making the much shorter distance to the pond.

The sheep farmer later had the idea of moving his flock down into the pasture to disguise the group's muddy footprints.

In order not to attract the attention of others during their ceremonies, Tarnhow-Miller began to circulate stories about the water spirits to keep people in at night. He even managed to find some discarded church records which referred to the mythical creature of the *Knucker Hole*. Over time, the superstitious locals began to refrain from walking anywhere near Goose Green after dark.

Our investigation into the death of Kathleen Tomkinson unsettled the group, who, until then, had believed that they could operate with relative impunity. Even the normally unflappable Tarnhow-Miller was unnerved by the questions being asked. He had been careful to distance himself from the others, taking no part in their deviant sexual practises, and being discreet in his purchase of the pendants. As a precaution, he sought to hide the robes and hoods, little realising that a small label on his own garment would be his undoing.

When the men were eventually tried, the case created headlines across the globe. Holmes and I received plaudits from Captain Drummond and his senior officers at a special ceremony arranged after the four members of *The Neckar* had been sentenced. Yet there was little sense of triumph in the aftermath, the pointless cruelty of the crimes leaving a nasty taste in all our mouths.

For PC Daubney, the case had a special significance. It served to earn him his promotion to sergeant, and within a year he had risen to the rank of inspector. For Holmes it was but another case to add to the Baker Street archive. He rarely mentioned the affair, save for those few occasions when he would retrieve a small box of trinkets from the mantlepiece and sift through its contents, his attention being drawn inevitably to the small silver pendant and its mermaid motif.

3. The Yuletide Heist

I have recounted more than once, that when the mood took him, my good friend Sherlock Holmes was something of a consummate storyteller. At such times, he would regale his listeners with narratives that were both gripping and puzzling. Most often, these were tales of adventure and intrigue in which he had played no small part. And it was in the December of 1896, that he chose to share with us one of his most absorbing stories – a mystery he referred to simply as *The Yuletide Heist*.

On the Christmas Eve of that year, we had a full house at 221B. Assisted by Billy, the page, Mrs. Hudson had spent the better part of the day preparing a veritable feast for our consumption that evening. Holmes had insisted that the pair should join the festivities at the large refectory table which had been assembled in the upstairs apartment. Alongside the four of us, the other invited guests included Inspectors Lestrade and Eastland from Scotland Yard; Dr. Henry Tamworth, an academic from King's College, Cambridge; and Mrs. Celina Grimble, a long-standing member of the Wandsworth Ladies' Reading Circle; with whom I had corresponded for some years. We were a disparate group to be sure, but the atmosphere and bonhomie that evening was both cheery and heart-warming.

Our meal had commenced with a piping hot dish of Palestine soup, made with delicious Jerusalem artichokes and a variety of exotic spices. The main course was a further Mrs. Hudson speciality, a lavish and extravagant serving of roasted goose with sage and onion stuffing, ham, potatoes, oysters, peas, and cabbage. And during the consumption of this, Holmes began his unusual narrative.

"I have often reflected," said he, "on the extraordinary lengths that some criminals will go to in perpetrating their felonious deeds. A simple and uncomplicated plan of action will often be discarded in favour of a more elaborate scheme designed to misdirect and unseat the most dogged of investigators. And yet, it is sometimes this particular or peculiar *over complication* which serves to expose the man or woman concerned."

"I'm not sure I follow," announced Inspector Giles Eastland, his round, chubby face flushed with a distinctly crimson hue which had no doubt been brought on by the three glasses of strong Madeira he had managed to consume since being seated at the table. "Are you saying that some criminals are too clever for their own good?"

Holmes eyed him keenly. "Yes, it is sometimes simply that. But there is more. It is often in the formulation of a most cunning plan that our offender leaves more tangible clues than he might otherwise. That was certainly true in the case of *The Tichborne Claimant*[1]. Arthur Orton's confession last year came as no surprise. Throughout his long and unsuccessful claim to be the missing heir to Sir Henry Tichborne's baronetcy, he devised a most fiendish and over-complicated back story to support his assertion. In my view, it

---

[1] The Tichborne case captivated the press and public in the 1860s and 1870s. Arthur Orton, a butcher's son from Wapping, claimed to be Roger Tichborne, who was believed to have been shipwrecked in 1854 on the passage to Australia. Responding to Lady Tichborne's advertisements in the Australian press, he came forward to claim the Tichborne inheritance in 1866, saying that he had been living under the name Thomas Castro and working as a butcher in the remote settlement of Wagga Wagga. While Lady Tichborne accepted him as her long lost son, his legal claim failed, and in 1874 he was convicted of perjury and sentenced to 14 years in prison. In 1895, he confessed to being Arthur Orton, although he later retracted this.

was this over-elaboration which ultimately enabled his scheme to be laid bare."

"I have to agree with you there," said Mrs. Grimble with some gusto. "Frightful man he was. And what a cock and bull story he told!"

There was some merriment at this, although Mrs. Hudson – who was sat beside her – seemed somewhat shocked by the remark and shot a glance at young Billy, who appeared to find the comment particularly humorous and had chortled loudly.

It was Inspector Lestrade who spoke next, raising his fork on which was still positioned a sizeable piece of goose meat. "I take the point, Mr. Holmes, but give me a straightforward case any day. A cleverly devised criminal enterprise may leave more by way of breadcrumbs, but always increases the amount of legwork that needs to be undertaken. Sometimes, we detectives have neither the time nor the energy to pursue such matters."

I believe I saw Holmes suppress a grin at this. "My dear Lestrade, it is in those more challenging and colourful cases that the greatest satisfaction is to be had. It is the very reason I set myself up as the world's first consulting detective!"

Mrs. Hudson beamed at Holmes as she passed a dish of roasted potatoes across to Dr. Tamworth. To this point, the aged and somewhat emaciated anatomist had said little, while eating a great deal, and now seemed intent on filling his plate for a second time. As a longstanding acquaintance of the great detective, he had often been invited to dine with us at Baker Street, and with a sharp wit and inherent curiosity about all of life's mysteries, had often proved to be an affable dinner guest. It was he who then addressed my colleague.

"Then tell us, Mr. Holmes, of all the cases that you have investigated over the years, what is the one single affair which most aptly illustrates your point? I would be keen to hear about a convoluted crime which was, by its nature, over-planned, to the extent that it enabled you to solve it more easily than you might otherwise."

"Me too!" opined Mrs. Grimble.

The nodding heads confirmed that we were all in agreement. With a distinct twinkle in his eye, Holmes began: "Well then, it seems I have little choice but to lay before you one of the most fascinating cases of my early career, in the days before the good doctor became my most trusted associate."

Mrs. Hudson gave me an approving nod and having taken a sip of her dry white sherry, settled back into the dining chair and fixed her gaze upon Holmes. Like the rest of us, she clearly relished the opportunity to hear the detective talk about a case in his own words. Beyond the flickering of the gas lamps and the gentle crackle of the seasoned logs burning merrily in the hearth, there was an expectant silence.

"I was still living in Montague Street in the December of 1878. The year had been a busy one, and as Christmas approached, I anticipated that my caseload might ease somewhat. Yet this was not to be the case. I became embroiled in two or three minor investigations in both the lead-up to the 25th of December and the few days beyond that. But it was on Friday, the 3rd of January of the following year, that I received an urgent telegram from a prestigious private bank on Victoria Street. For reasons of confidentiality, I will refrain from naming the institution concerned.

"In short, the bank wished me to investigate the circumstances surrounding a most audacious heist. A sizeable sum of cash had been stolen from an elaborately protected bank vault which sat one floor beneath the bank's three-storey building. The robbery had been planned to allow the thieves the maximum amount of time between taking the money, and the point at which the loss of the cash would be discovered. The bank had placed the last deposits in the vault on the 23rd of December, and, having closed for the Christmas and New Year period, it was only on the morning of the 3rd of January that the vault was reopened and the crime detected. The thieves had, therefore, a full ten days to cover their tracks after pulling off the heist.

"In the scheme of things, the bank considered this to be a significant, yet surprisingly manageable, loss. While the vault had contained around five to six hundred locked safety deposit boxes – containing jewellery and other assets estimated to value more than £5 million – it was clear that none of these had been tampered with. The thieves had confined themselves to the carefully stacked bundles of banknotes which sat on a central plinth on the floor of the vault. And yet, even here, their ambitions had been conservative. While the vault held more than £1 million in cash deposits, of various currencies and denominations from around the world, the gang had taken only £100,000 in sterling banknotes. Given this situation, the bank was keen to avoid any sort of public scandal and desired only to prevent its depositors from withdrawing their cash and other assets, which would effectively plunge the business into liquidation. The directors believed that they could make some accounting adjustments to cover the loss and took the decision *not* to call the police. However, they could not risk the same thing happening again, so they called me in to determine how the heist had been executed, so that steps could be taken to strengthen the bank's security arrangements and prevent any future robberies."

At this point, Holmes paused to raise a glass of cabernet sauvignon to his lips to refresh his palate. Inspector Lestrade took the opportunity to interject, his pinched and drawn features hiding none of his disdain for what he had just heard. "It is disappointing to learn that a prestigious financial institution would choose to conduct its affairs in such a way. I mean no slur on your abilities and credentials, Mr. Holmes, but a crime of this magnitude should surely have warranted the attentions of Scotland Yard's finest."

Inspector Eastland nodded in agreement, but Holmes refused to be drawn too far down that path. "I take your point, gentlemen, but I had little choice but to accede to my client's terms for carrying out the investigation. I must admit that I was a little surprised when I arrived at the bank around ten o'clock that morning to find no police presence. In fact, beyond the half dozen bank staff and directors who knew of the robbery, there was only one other person present – an engineer from the firm which had installed the locking mechanism of the solidly constructed vault door. He had been called in at short notice to ascertain whether the lock had failed or had been tampered with in any way."

My own curiosity was piqued by this. "So, had it? It seems clear to me that some simple form of lock-picking would be the most obvious way to steal from the vault, having gained access to the building."

Holmes smiled. "If only the solution had been that straightforward. But the engineer was completely baffled. He said that the mechanism appeared to have worked exactly as it should have done and could see no way in which the thieves could have entered the vault. To understand the significance of this, I will explain how the elaborate security system worked.

"Firstly, we start with the building itself. The ground floor foyer consisted of a large open area in which were situated the front desk and counters used by the bank staff, a toilet, and a few ancillary storage rooms. While there were large windows on both sides of this space, they were set high up in the room and could not be opened. All were intact and showed no signs of having been interfered with when examined that Friday morning. The entrance to the foyer was through two large front doors which faced onto Victoria Street. At night, and during the weekends, a uniformed concierge would sit at a desk to the side of these doors. Two men were employed for this task, sharing the different shifts between them. Stanley Bliss, the elder of the two, had been with the bank for more than twenty years. His counterpart, Harley Coulter, had been employed for a little under ten months. Alongside the bank's manager and under-manager, they were the only staff that held keys to the front entrance door and other areas of the building. There were no other doors to the property, and my subsequent investigations showed that all of the locks to the doors and bolts to the windows of the building were intact and working as they should."

Inspector Eastland spluttered in response to this. "Now, there's a telling clue, right there! My intuition tells me that the newer man was at the centre of this. Without keys, there could be no heist. There would be no way of gaining access to the vault." He shifted heavily on his chair and took in a deep breath.

"I'm not sure I agree," said Mrs. Grimble somewhat brusquely. "I've been reading crime and mystery books for some years since I first discovered *The Moonstone* by Wilkie Collins, and I never miss one of Dr. Watson's publications. At this stage in the narrative, there could be other ways in which the robbers gained access to the locked vault; an underground tunnel, maybe, the use of explosives, or perhaps by leaving someone on the inside who could then open the vault door and reset the locking mechanism after the cash was stolen."

Eastland seemed unable or unwilling to respond to this challenge and reached once more for his Madeira glass. Holmes sought to respond to both sets of comments.

"These are exactly the sort of considerations that occurred to me that wintry morning. But let me tell you more about the security and the vault itself. It will help to address some of the splendid ideas suggested by Mrs. Grimble. A locked door at the back of the foyer provided access to all the other areas of the building; a staircase to the upper floors and a slope leading down to the vault room. Further locked doors provided access to all the corridors of the upper floors, and it was the bank's policy to ensure that every single room throughout the building had an individual lock and marked key and was always secured when the members of the staff were not at work. This included a final locked door which stood at the entrance to the vault room."

It was the bright-eyed and fresh-faced Billy who then spoke. "Please excuse the interruption, sir, but I just wanted to be clear. If the thieves had wanted to get to and from the vault using the Victoria Street entrance, they would have required three different keys."

"That is a perfect summary, my young friend."

"And all of that before they could even attempt to open the vault."

"Indeed."

"Well, Mr. Holmes, that does suggest that one of the concierges had to be involved. Sat behind the doors to one side, he could not have failed to see the robbers enter."

"Billy, we will make a detective of you yet! I was about to tell you more about the vault, but your polite interruption is a timely one, for I should have said more about the responsibilities of the concierge. On any working day, the bank closed its doors to customers at three-thirty in the afternoon. Staff working at the bank would then spend time reconciling all the day's transactions, typically leaving for home at five o'clock. For a further hour, the building would be occupied by only the manager and under-manager. During that time, they would be responsible for locking the vault and securing the two doors back to the main foyer. At a few minutes before six o'clock, the concierge would arrive at work, using his own keys to enter the building. He would then wait for the manager and under-manager to appear in the foyer before commencing work. When the two managers had left for the evening, the concierge would be the only person left in the building."

"This is lending more weight to my colleague's assertion that one of the uniformed men must have been involved," said Inspector Lestrade, giving a sly wink to Eastland, who looked to perk up a little at the show of support.

"We will come to that," replied Holmes, with just the merest hint of agitation in his voice. First, let me continue with the routine observed by the concierge. During the first hour, he would check all the doors on each floor, starting with the door to the vault. While he would never expect to find this unlocked, it was quite common for some of the doors on the upper floors to be left unlocked as staff departed for the evening. The bank was a stickler for routines and paperwork. Ticking off his progress using a printed checklist, the concierge was required to approach every door, and check that nothing was amiss in each room. This included checking that all the windows were firmly secured. Having to unlock and relock so many doors was time-consuming but necessary, as far as the bank was concerned. Until the heist, it had never experienced any form of break-in. This routine of checking would be repeated twice more during the night – once at ten o'clock, with a final tour of the building at four the following morning. Each tour would take a minimum of forty-five minutes. Stanley Bliss admitted that he and his colleague were never in a hurry to complete the task as it broke up the monotony of the ten-hour shift."

"During which time, the front entrance was left unattended and exposed," opined Mrs. Hudson, frowning with some disapproval.

Holmes nodded in agreement. "Yes, for all the bank's well-planned procedures, this was a clear area of weakness. Anyone with a knowledge of the routine would realise that they had three periods of at least forty-five minutes in which they could enter and leave the building with little risk of detection."

I could not help but interject: "And, of those, the ten o'clock and four o'clock slots would be preferrable, given that the normally busy Victoria Street would be much quieter."

"That was my working assumption."

Dr. Tamworth, who had been listening most attentively, was clearly convinced by the emerging hypothesis, but appeared eager to get the heart of the matter. "That all sounds credible but does not address the issue of the allegedly corrupt concierge. Someone on the inside must have been involved to allow the thieves to gain access to the three keys needed to get to the vault. If we are convinced that the bank managers were innocent, then it must have been one of the two uniformed men."

"Not necessarily," answered Mrs. Grimble, once again playing devil's advocate. "Any of the four sets of keys we have been told about could have been copied and placed in the hands of the criminals. Furthermore, this could have been done with or without the knowledge of the key holder. They may have been stolen for that purpose and replaced before the loss was realised."

Inspector Eastland was having none of it. "That's a lot of keys that would need to be cut."

Mrs. Grimble was quick to react: "No, just the three. As Billy observed so eloquently, only three keys were needed to get from the front entrance to the door of the vault."

Billy piped up in support of the bespectacled Mrs. Grimble. "Yes, and Mr. Holmes said that all of the keys were 'marked'. I took that to mean that they could be individually identified according to which lock they were supposed to fit." He looked across at Holmes who was pleased to nod in confirmation.

"The keys were indeed marked – etched with some numbers and letters according to the floor and room concerned. This made it easier for the three specific keys to be identified and copied away from the bank."

Inspector Lestrade seemed surprised at the revelation. "So, it wasn't one of the concierges who let the thieves in on the night of the raid?"

"Not as such. It was later to become clear that the robbery had occurred on Christmas Eve. Stanley Bliss had been on duty that night. As far as the bank was concerned, he was beyond suspicion given his dedicated years of service. My subsequent investigations cleared him of any involvement. And while it would have been tempting to believe that the more recently employed Harley Coulter had acted in concert with the felons, this also proved not to be the case. On the night in question, Coulter had a solid alibi. He had visited some relatives in Lincolnshire and had stopped overnight at an hotel in Scunthorpe. No, our inside man proved to be none other than Dominic Tuttle, the former concierge whom Harley Coulter had replaced. Before leaving the job, he had three duplicate keys cut to enable the robbers to reach the vault. I will explain how we netted him a little later. For the moment, let us turn to the vault itself.

"In the room designated, the bank had installed the most sophisticated and expensive vault locking system on the market at that time, designed and built by a prestigious Swiss clock manufacturer. The door had no keys or combination locks. It was opened, instead, by a clockwork mechanism housed on the inside of the door. Once set, it could not be tampered with and had been built to withstand both heavy drilling and explosive charges. Each evening, the manager and under-manager would set the timer on the inside of the door and, where required, ensure that the clockwork mechanism was wound to the correct point. The timer would be set for a period of up to twelve days and was fixed to open only at eight o'clock on the chosen morning. Once the door had been closed it could not be unlocked until that time. The lock was serviced once a year and the timing mechanism adjusted accordingly. In its ten years of service, it had never failed or lost more than a fraction of a second in time. It was a remarkable piece of engineering."

Mrs. Grimble looked a little crestfallen. "So, my ideas about tunnels and people being left in the vault can be discounted then, Mr. Holmes?"

"Yes, on this occasion. The vault had remained intact and there was nothing to suggest that anyone had been hidden in the space. However, it might interest you to learn that the door could be opened from the inside. It was a failsafe mechanism built in to prevent one of the bank staff inadvertently locking themselves in. However, given the responsibility placed on those setting and locking the door, this task was never left to anyone other than the manager and under-manager in concert who would double check the settings. When I first arrived at the bank, they gave me every assurance that there had been no one inside the vault when the door was shut on the evening of the 23rd of December."

"Well, that's a pretty mystery then!" said a smiling Dr. Tamworth. "You said earlier that the engineer who was called in on the morning of the 3rd of January could find nothing wrong. That being the case, I can see no logical way in which the safe could have been opened prior to that."

"Nor I," agreed Mrs. Hudson. "Now, I'm sure we are all eager to learn more Mr. Holmes, but could Billy and I be allowed a short amount of time to clear the plates and serve afters? I have a steamed plum pudding with brandy for those that still have the space. And if your appetite is more limited, there are cranberry and mince pies."

There was an enthusiastic response to the housekeeper's announcement. My colleague agreed to a short interval, and while the plates were cleared and the desserts served, most of the menfolk took the opportunity to have a smoke in front of the fire. I spent the time talking to Mrs. Grimble about some of the cases we had been engaged in earlier that year, including *The Disappearance of Lady Frances Carfax, The Veiled Lodger* and *The Sussex Vampire*. She was also fascinated to learn that we had finally brought to justice a certain Edwin Halvergate, one of Professor Moriarty's long-standing foot soldiers, who had taken it upon himself to lead what remained of the academic's criminal fraternity in the wake of the events at the Reichenbach Falls.

It was approaching eight-thirty that evening when the dessert plates had finally been cleared and a few gifts that had been hanging on the Christmas tree were distributed to our guests. With everyone's glass replenished with their favourite seasonal tipple, Holmes resumed his narrative.

"As you might imagine, I used the first couple of hours at the bank to interview all the relevant staff and directors and to conduct a thorough inspection of the building, paying particular attention to the vault and all the areas leading to it. Given that he had already completed his work in examining the locking mechanism, I also took the opportunity to quiz Alex Dunlop, the vault engineer, before he departed."

"Aha!" said Inspector Lestrade, with a knowing look on his face. "Very wise, I'd say. In your position, I'd have done the same, to find out more about the annual service."

"Indeed. And a very fruitful line of enquiry it proved to be. For Dunlop had *not* been the engineer who had carried out the routine maintenance two days prior to the Christmas shutdown. In fact, he had never visited the bank before the 3rd of January, and had only been called in to assist as the regular engineer, Frank Chilvers, had failed to show up for work that morning."

"Highly suspicious," agreed Inspector Eastland, now resembling the deep hue of the port he was imbibing at some pace.

"Yes, but that wasn't the only irregularity. Dunlop had checked the firm's maintenance records before setting off for the bank. Frank Chilvers had signed off on the completion of the annual service, but his maintenance log was inaccurate."

Mrs. Grimble was as fascinated as the rest of us. "In what sense?"

"As far as the records were concerned, the work required a single engineer, but when quizzed, the manager and under-manager confirmed that the annual service had been undertaken by two engineers. In fact, when I asked about this, the two men had to concede that it had been unusual. In ten years, they had never known the task to require more than one person. The under-manager then recalled that Chilvers had mentioned something about the second engineer being 'an apprentice' and recollected that the young man in question had looked extremely youthful, if not a little effeminate. He remembered seeing the lad struggling to wheel in the trolley which carried the large toolbox the engineers brought with them for the service."

"That is extremely suggestive but serves only to further complicate our attempt to unpick the *method* by which this crime was carried out," replied the ardent crime reader. "And how did you act on this additional information, Mr. Holmes?"

The detective gave Mrs. Grimble the broadest of smiles. "My investigations then required me to leave the bank and put in some good, old-fashioned, legwork. I will be honest in saying that my inspection of the building yielded no further clues. The thieves appeared to have been extremely diligent in covering their tracks. Not so much as a hair, footprint or fingerprint had been left in the vault."

"Fingerprint, Mr. Holmes?!" said Billy, with a look of some confusion. "Why would you look for a fingerprint?"

Somewhat to the surprise of those around the table, it was Dr. Tamworth who answered. "I am sure that Mr. Holmes will forgive me, but this is an area of study I have long been interested in. Marcello Malpighi, a professor of anatomy at the University of Bologna, was the first to identify the ridges, spirals and loops that define the nature of fingerprints, as far back as 1686. In 1788, another anatomist, the German

Johann Mayer, concluded that fingerprints are unique to each individual. More recently, academics and law enforcement agencies have sought to develop classification systems for identifying and recording them. When we have a workable system, it should be possible to match any prints taken from the scene of a crime to the recorded fingerprints of the criminal involved."

Inspector Eastland looked unconvinced and Lestrade merely rolled his eyes before commenting. "Yes, but he didn't find any fingerprints, so that wouldn't have been much use."

Mrs. Grimble seemed to find this exchange amusing, but pressed Holmes further. "Come on, Mr. Holmes, we want to know what happened next?!"

"Well, my enquiries the next day were focused on locating the whereabouts of Frank Chilvers, the lock engineer, and Dominic Tuttle, the former concierge. The bank provided me with an address for the latter, which proved to be a shabby two-up, two-down house in Shoreditch. The landlady of the property informed me that Tuttle had lived there for about three years but had announced before Christmas that he was moving out and did so just two days later. She was not at all pleased, particularly as Tuttle refused to say where he was moving to when asked about a forwarding address for any post he might receive."

Mrs. Hudson smiled broadly. "I'm sure that the landlady *did* find out where he was heading. There isn't much that escapes the notice of a good housekeeper."

"How right you are, Mrs. Hudson! For the very meticulous landlady had occasion to observe some papers while dusting in her lodger's room on the day before he departed. It seems he had already purchased a ticket for the Train Ferry crossing from Dover to Calais and had made arrangements for the onward rail journey to Paris where he was booked to stay at the Hôtel de Lalande."

"Very neat," observed Inspector Eastland, "and awfully expensive, no doubt. So, I imagine you were thinking that Tuttle had to be one of the thieves, who had arranged to escape to the Continent after the heist and before the robbery was discovered?"

"That was one of my thoughts. The other was that Tuttle had been paid handsomely for supplying the duplicate keys and had made the arrangements knowing he was likely to be investigated as a former concierge. Either way, his actions served only to highlight his probable complicity. In my view, an unnecessary *over complication*. Had he continued to reside in Shoreditch and had refuted any suggestion that he had supplied the keys, there would have been little that I could have done to bring him to justice. Try as I might, I could never prove where he had arranged for the keys to be cut.

"So, for the moment, we will leave our comfortably accommodated Mr. Tuttle in his Parisian hotel room and turn instead to Frank Chilvers. His firm had an office and workshop in Clerkenwell from which it carried out services and repairs to the wide variety of clockwork mechanisms the Swiss-owned business had installed across the capital. Chilvers was in his mid-thirties and had worked there for over a decade. He was a trusted employee. I visited the office the day after the robbery had been discovered. The firm's fears that Chilvers may have had a hand in the robbery had grown when the man failed to appear at work for a second day. A work colleague had then been sent to Chilvers's rented property in Farringdon, but found it empty, and had no success in discovering the engineer's whereabouts. I was a little more fortunate.

"My enquiries at the office in Clerkenwell revealed two pieces of information which proved to be crucial. The first was that he had graduated from Cambridge with a first-class honours degree in engineering. As well as being a talented engineer, the man was highly literate and able to speak a variety of European languages, skills which his Swiss employer valued a great deal. The second was that he had romantic inclinations towards a young lady he had been reacquainted with eighteen months earlier. His work colleagues knew only that her name was 'Ellen Cox,' for Chilvers had always been tight-lipped about revealing anything further of the woman."

"Aha!" squealed Mrs. Grimble. "We have our romantic interest! Like any good mystery story, there has to be some amorous element."

Once again, Mrs. Hudson looked troubled by the lady's outburst and I saw her calmly, yet surreptitiously, move the carafe of Madeira away from Mrs. Grimble's immediate grasp as Holmes continued his narrative.

"Having returned briefly to my rooms in Montague Street, I then travelled up to Cambridge by rail that afternoon to visit this Ellen Cox."

"How did you know she lived in Cambridge?" I asked, incredulously. "You had but her name."

"I believed that if Chilvers had been *reacquainted* with the young lady, there was every likelihood that the pair met originally when Chilvers was a student. Working on the basis that the woman might still reside in Cambridge, I consulted my collection of street directories for the town and had a lucky break. There was an entry for a Miss Ellen Cox in one of the directories, which showed that she was the owner of a private residence close to Appleton Meadows on the outskirts of Cambridge."

"A very desirable area in which to live," announced Dr. Tamworth. "I wish my academic salary afforded me such a location."

"Yes," replied Holmes. "Appleton Meadows is an open space to the south of Cambridge, which sits alongside the River Cam. It is a popular destination for students, hikers and naturalists – many of the latter being drawn to the marshy woodland areas which host species like the butterbur and musk beetle."

"Very picturesque, I'm sure," intoned Inspector Lestrade, "but let's hear more about your visit to the young lady and how this led you to Chilvers."

Holmes was not ruffled by the gruff remark. "Well, a fifteen-minute cart ride took me from the railway station to the pretty village of Appleton. And it did not take me too long to locate the property, named – appropriately enough – *Appleton House*. It was a sizeable building, created in the early part of the century; square in shape, attractive in design, and covering a plot of maybe five acres, the highlight of which was a broad rectangle of land which stretched down to, and gave unparalleled views of, the meadows themselves.

"A young servant girl greeted me at the door and took my card when I announced that I wished to speak to Miss Cox. A few minutes later I was shown into the spacious parlour of the property where I was met by a smiling, albeit slightly bemused, woman in her early thirties. She was around five feet four inches in height, with a delicate, pale complexion, and bright blue eyes. The braided buns of her light blonde hair suggested that she might have been of Scandinavian descent, but the clear, clipped tones of her diction gave no hint of a foreign accent. She wore a simple powder blue dress with a high neckline, over which she had fastened a thick tartan shawl with a brooch resembling a scarab beetle.

"The lady directed me towards a comfortable armchair close to the fire and instructed the maid to prepare a pot of tea for us, before taking a seat on a sofa opposite me. She then asked: 'How may I help you, Mr. Holmes? Your card says you are a *private detective*. I don't think I have ever met one of those before.'

"I smiled. 'Indeed, Miss Cox. You will have to forgive my impromptu visit to your beautiful home, but this is a matter of some urgency. I am trying to locate the whereabouts of a man I believe you know – a Mr. Frank Chilvers.'

"The statement had an immediate and telling effect. Miss Cox shifted in her chair and brought her hands together tightly. She blinked three or four times and then sought to regain her composure. 'Frank Chilvers? Yes, I did know a man by that name some years ago. We met at the university. Frank was studying at the school of engineering, while I had permission to attend some mathematics lectures given by a friend of my father's, even though I was not formally recognised as an undergraduate. I will be candid, Mr. Holmes. We did walk out together for some months, but when my father found out he forbade me from seeing or speaking to Frank, whom he considered to be an unsuitable match.'

"'And why was that if you do not mind me asking?'

"She responded confidently. 'I was always due to inherit a small fortune. My great-great-grandfather was a successful jeweller, and both my father and grandfather continued in the same vein, bringing further wealth to the family. However, as an only child, the line stopped with me. My father was overprotective and wanted to ensure that the man I married was my social equal. Frank was the son of a carpenter, and while he was a gifted engineer set for a good career, had still to make his way in the world. My father believed that if he married me, he would have no incentive to do so, and would shirk his responsibilities, relying on my inheritance. Something he told Frank in no uncertain terms. After his graduation, we went our separate ways. I took a job at a private school for girls, while Frank moved to London to work for an engineering firm.'

"'And have you seen him since that time,' I then asked.

"This time her reply seemed a little less assured. 'No. I have lived here at *Appleton House* all of my life. My mother died when I was but six years of age. Father passed away four years ago, leaving me the house and the family inheritance. And I have been alone since that time. I have had no cause to contact Frank and I imagine he would feel the same.'

"While we drank our tea, she asked why I was trying to contact Chilvers. I had no desire to reveal my hand, so made no mention of the bank heist, saying only that he had failed to turn up for work and his employer had been concerned as to his whereabouts. The explanation seemed to placate her, for she made no further mention of the man and the conversation drifted on to other topics. A short while later, I thanked her for her time and said that I would need to find a way of returning to the railway station. Her face took on a look of some concern, as she explained that I was unlikely to find any sort of cab, cart, or carriage in the vicinity. She then suggested I might like to walk through to the bottom of her garden, where I would find a footpath running through the meadows alongside the river which provided a direct and most charming route back to the town. I agreed to do so.

"We left the parlour and walked through the house towards the rear of the property. As we did so, we passed a large, brightly lit, study to my right. Inside I could see tables, cabinets, shelves, and plinths displaying many clocks, automata, and other mechanical devices. I was at once intrigued and asked her about them. She explained that the collection had belonged to her great, great, grandfather, and she could not bear to part with them. I stared into the room for some time, deep in thought, before turning to see that Miss Cox was regarding me keenly.

"'A fascinating collection,'" said I, trying to play down my elation at seeing the devices.

"'Indeed. An inheritance like none other,'" she replied rather enigmatically.

"At the rear of the house we passed into a large, glass domed, conservatory filled with exotic plants from across the globe. A small wood-burning stove had been placed to one side to keep the plants at an acceptable temperature even in the depths of an English winter. Miss Cox unlocked some double doors at the far end of the conservatory, and we stepped into the garden.

"The view which greeted me was as perfect as it was engineered. An exquisitely ordered arrangement of borders, beds, and pergolas, down the centre of which ran a broad lawn with not so much as a hint of a weed. Beyond the vista of the garden was a panoramic view of Appleton Meadows in all their natural glory. The contrast between the two could not have been more distinct.

"In the very epicentre of the formal garden was a circular area of lawn in the middle of which sat a large brass sundial. As we passed the timepiece, I saw Miss Cox extend her right hand to touch the dial, gently, and fleetingly, with obvious affection. A gesture which I imagined she always did when passing by.

"At the very end of the garden was a small gate to the left, which placed me on a path leading down to the river's edge and the route back to Cambridge. I thanked Miss Cox for her time and set off at a pace, eager to make it to the railway station as quickly as I could for the journey back to London. With what I knew, I could afford to waste no further time."

There seemed to be some confusion in the room at this point, and it was young Billy who voiced the concern we all appeared to share. "I don't understand what you learnt from Miss Cox, sir. While she admitted to knowing Frank Chilvers, she said she had not seen him since his student days. Even if she had been lying, I cannot see how that would have helped you to find the engineer."

"You have a splendid enquiring mind, Billy," Holmes retorted. "But I think you have failed to realise why the encounter with Miss Cox was so revealing."

"He's not the only one," admitted Mrs. Grimble. "I think I must have missed something too!"

Inspector Lestrade smiled broadly and sought to explain. "I think what Mr. Holmes is trying to say, is that Miss Cox's reaction to his appearance was odd and very telling. In fact, it wasn't a *reaction* at all. Not once did she ask Mr. Holmes *how* he came to know of her and her connection to Frank Chilvers. And if it had been true that she hadn't had any contact with the engineer for many years, she would surely have asked Mr. Holmes *why* he wished to know. I'm guessing that the moment she saw the card announcing that a *private detective* wished to speak to her, she knew someone was on to Frank Chilvers. By implication, this suggests that she already knew of the bank robbery."

Holmes agreed. "From my earlier enquiries, and what I had subsequently seen in the house, I knew that Miss Cox had to be involved. And I was already speculating that the bright young woman was likely to be the architect of the heist. I just had to find out why."

Inspector Eastland was clearly struggling to keep up. "How could you possibly believe that she was involved given what you've told us?"

It was Mrs. Hudson who answered, with some satisfaction. "Inspector Eastland, remember the *apprentice* engineer who helped Frank Chilvers to service the locking mechanism? That wasn't an effeminate young man, it was Ellen Cox herself!"

"Indeed, Mrs. Hudson. "Her role was pivotal, as I will clarify shortly. But let me first explain what happened next. I returned to London in the early evening and made my way to the Diogenes Club, an establishment frequented by my older brother, Mycroft. As some of you in the room will know, my brother has a fair degree of influence within government and diplomatic circles. I told him about the robbery and explained the nature of my quest. Principally, that I needed the French authorities to arrest Frank Chilvers and Dominic Tuttle at the Hôtel de Lalande and have them returned to England. I could not risk letting Ellen Cox get a message to them saying that their robbery had been exposed."

"How did you know that Chilvers had joined Tuttle in fleeing to France?" asked Dr. Tamworth.

"I did not know for certain but believed that to be the most logical outcome. Like Tuttle, Chilvers had already cleared out of his rented property. It would make sense for the two to travel together on the pre-arranged journey and to hide out in France."

"I disagree," said Mrs. Grimble. "Surely they would have been taking a most extraordinary risk, having carried out the robbery, and being in possession of some or all of the stolen cash?"

"No," came the reply. "They would not have risked that. I conjectured that the proceeds of the robbery would be left in safe hands. Namely, those of Ellen Cox, who would no doubt return to Cambridgeshire to hide the loot. Having done so, it was then simply a matter of waiting until the coast was clear and getting word to her two accomplices that it was safe for them to return to England."

There was general hubbub in the room after this, with everyone voicing their thoughts and ideas. It took my colleague some moments to regain his ground and to continue with the narrative: "My plans worked to perfection. Mycroft's rapid intervention, and hastily arranged telegrams to his counterparts in France, yielded the desired results. Early the next morning, both Chilvers and Tuttle were detained by officers from the Paris Police Prefecture. By the evening of the same day, they were on the Train Ferry back to England in the custody of two burly officials from the British Embassy. Having arrived back in London, they were placed under house arrest in the Farringdon property which Chilvers had vacated some days earlier."

"Did they admit to the crime?" asked Billy eagerly.

"No. I visited them the following day and explained that I was investigating the robbery on behalf of the bank. Both men refused to say anything. Chilvers even questioned the legality of the house arrest."

Inspector Eastland had an opinion on this. "I don't mean to sound churlish, Mr. Holmes, but he had a point. Under what powers were you acting? Did you involve Scotland Yard after all?"

Holmes brushed aside the concern. "The arrangements were made by the Home Office. As the men had refused to give a clear account of why they had travelled to France, they were being detained as suspected spies. In fact, a mysterious note found in the possession of Frank Chilvers gave some credence to the notion that they were withholding information. It was one of Mycroft's ruses, of course, but it gave me time to resolve all of the outstanding queries in the case."

"That's a little sneaky, Mr. Holmes!" said Dr. Tamworth, relishing the tale.

"True. But everything began to fall into place very quickly after that. My investigations into Ellen Cox's financial affairs revealed some startling information. After she had inherited the house and the financial legacy from her father, she had invested most of her wealth in some schemes suggested by her bank. Apparently knowing little of the nature of these investment schemes – which mainly involved risky overseas property ventures – she sustained substantial losses. The bank which advised her was none other than my client."

Mrs. Grimble clearly had a penchant for melodrama: "So, the robbery was an act of revenge!"

"I'm not sure I would put it quite like that. But her losses stood at around £100,000 – the same amount stolen from the vault during the raid."

"How extraordinary!" said I, every bit as enthralled as the others. "But if that was the motivation, how the devil did they carry out the heist? I still don't see how they managed to open the vault door."

Holmes was relishing the denouement. "That, of course, was the really clever aspect of the case. To understand the method, we must first delve back into Ellen Cox's family history. The room full of clocks, automata, and other mechanical devices I had seen at *Appleton House* had indeed been owned by the young lady's great, great, grandfather. But these were no mere ornaments. They had been crafted and engineered by the man himself. When I first saw them, I knew that her relative had to be the famous *James Cox*. She was being evasive in describing him as a 'successful jeweller.' In fact, James Cox was a jeweller, goldsmith, inventor, and entrepreneur, famous for producing elaborate and expensive automata like the *Peacock Clock*, a large automaton showcasing three life-sized mechanical birds. The clock was eventually bought by Catherine the Great, the Empress of Russia, in 1781.

"More significant than any of these creations, was his construction of a timepiece in the 1760s which he claimed to be a perpetual motion machine. Working in collaboration with a man named John Merlin, Cox created a clock which needed no winding. The device was powered by changes in atmospheric pressure, which resulted in the movement of the clock's winding mechanism. It was sufficient to enable the timepiece to run indefinitely, and a clever safety mechanism prevented any overwinding of the machine. The source of the clock's energy was a large barometer containing 150 lbs. of mercury."

Dr. Tamworth was quick to respond. "That's correct. I have read accounts of the timepiece, but while I am no expert in this field, believe I am right in saying that the clock was not a true perpetual motion machine, for its operation defied the laws of thermodynamics."

This was all too much for Inspector Eastland who looked as if he were about to suffer a fatal seizure. "Thermo...what?!" he spluttered, "scientific mumbo-jumbo! What's this got to do with the bank robbery?"

There was general hilarity at the officer's outburst. Even Lestrade allowed himself a loud guffaw in response. As Mrs. Hudson filled my brandy glass for a second time, Holmes sought to clarify things.

"In the bank, on that first day of the investigation, I began to speculate on the nature of the vault's lock. And it occurred to me that if the existing clockwork mechanism had been overridden in some way, the door could then have been primed to open at a time different to that set by the bank's manager and under manager. But my problem was one of power. Without the clockwork mechanism, or some form of alternative gas or electrical power, the timer would not have worked. But having seen Ellen Cox's display of timepieces, the solution presented itself. What if the clockwork mechanism had been overridden and replaced, instead, by something resembling *Cox's Timepiece*?"

As ever, Billy was quick to point out an obvious anomaly. "Yes, but when the vault engineer was called to the bank on the day the robbery was discovered, he said he could find nothing wrong with the lock. How could that be the case?"

Holmes's face lit up, as if he had been anticipating just such a challenge. "He found nothing wrong, because the clockwork mechanism had been restored to its original function."

Mrs. Grimble seemed unconvinced. "Then I'm as confused as ever. First you say the mechanism was tampered with, now you are saying it was fine. Which was it?!"

"Actually both," admitted Holmes. "My theory was this. Two days before the bank's Christmas shutdown, Chilvers had arranged for the annual service. While presented to the bank as an *apprentice*, Chilvers's very capable assistant was Ellen Cox. Having grown up surrounded by her great-great-grandfather's mechanical contraptions, she knew as much as there was to know about the operation of his famous mercury powered timepiece. I speculated that Ellen had become reacquainted with Chilvers following the death of her father, possibly after learning that her investments had gone sour. When Chilvers told her that he was responsible for servicing the bank's elaborate locking system, the two hatched a plan. Between them, they constructed a smaller and much lighter version of *Cox's Timepiece*, which could be housed temporarily within the space ordinarily occupied by the vault's clockwork mechanism. They had plenty of time to plan for this, and it was well within reason to imagine that Chilvers had copied all the required blueprints to engineer the replacement lock with complete precision.

"It was my belief that the heavy trolley which the *apprentice* had been seen to be struggling with was carrying the newly constructed timepiece hidden within what looked like a large toolbox. During the service itself, the couple removed all the superfluous clockwork components, hiding them in the toolbox. They then installed the new timepiece, powered by its mercury barometer. What was left of the original lock was set to deceive. It could still be wound up as before and the clock could still be set. But while the bank's managers believed they were setting the clock for the 3rd of January, this had no effect. The mercury timepiece was now controlling the operation of the lock with its own timer. The would-be thieves had set the door to open for two days at eight o'clock in the morning, consistent with the normal routine at the bank. But the third, and final, unlocking was set to occur on Christmas Eve when the heist would take place.

"It was then a matter of carrying out a successful robbery. We already know how the thieves entered the building. Chilvers would have met Dominic Tuttle on the many occasions he had visited the bank to carry out the annual service. It was probably the simple inducement of money which persuaded Tuttle to go along with the plan.

"With the concierge elsewhere in the building, they would have gone straight to the vault with the trolley carrying their tools and the clockwork parts removed earlier. And with the door now open, the three would have stuck to their assigned tasks given the limited time available. As the non-technical member of the gang, I imagine Dominic Tuttle was responsible for bagging up the money. Ellen Cox most likely focused on removing the mercury timepiece and placing it on the trolley. Frank Chilvers would then have used his expertise to replace all the original clockwork components. With this being the lengthiest part of the operation, I envisaged that Cox and Tuttle would use the time to wheel the trolley back to the entrance door of the bank carrying both the cash and the timepiece. And when Chilvers had completed his work, the lock could be reset to open on the 3rd of January. Beyond that, they had but to lock the entrance door behind them and wheel their trolley to the cart or carriage they had arrived in. In many respects, an almost perfect heist."

Inspector Lestrade had to concede. "Well, Mr. Holmes. I must agree with you. If your theory proved to be correct, this was indeed an unnecessarily *over-complicated* affair. But I'm fascinated to know how you *proved* any of it. With your detainees refusing to say anything and Ellen Cox still sitting on the stolen cash, what proof had you?"

"You are quite correct. That was my final challenge. Having crafted such an elaborate plan, I knew that Ellen Cox would have taken every precaution in hiding the cash until it was safe to retrieve it. And yet, once again, it was her over-thinking of the arrangements which proved to be her downfall. I mentioned earlier that when Frank Chilvers had been arrested in France, he was found to be in possession of a mysterious note. Mycroft had the document sent on to me, and it proved to be the one final piece of information I needed to crack the case. The typed note read as follows:

...Whispering whirls of water flow, down winding willowed waterways, as seasoned sun soothes shallow depths, of summer's silent stream...

Mrs. Grimble could barely contain her delight. "Such beautiful alliteration, and so evocative. This has certainly proved to be a most entertaining mystery, Mr. Holmes, but what did it mean?!"

"The note was still contained within its envelope – one that had been sent from England on the 27th of December 1878 and addressed to Chilvers at the Hôtel de Lalande. It was postmarked *Appleton*."

Billy was quick on the uptake. "Then it was a coded message from Ellen Cox!"

"Yes. I was later to find out from the lady herself that it was part of a love poem written for her by Chilvers after his first visit to *Appleton House*, way back in the summer of 1866 when the two had first met. It took me some time to work out the full significance of the extract, for it was a clever attempt at concealment..."

To my surprise, it was Mrs. Hudson who interposed. "Forgive me, sir, but I believe I know what the note was meant to convey. The extract was to remind Chilvers of their shared time together all those years ago, but, more specifically, was telling him that the stolen cash had been successfully hidden – somewhere close to Appleton Meadows!"

There was a round of applause and much raising of glasses in salute to the housekeeper's proclamation. Holmes was ebullient in his reply: "Capital, Mrs. Hudson! But there was more. The note communicated the *precise* location of the plunder, for it contained directions to the hole in which both the cash and the mercury powered timepiece had been buried within a sealed metal strongbox. I realised that the alliteration of the poem had been used to great effect, given the predominance of 'W's and 'S's at the start of most of the words. In fact, there are six 'W's and seven 'S's. I concluded that these were compass directions from a given point; six feet 'West' and seven feet 'South'. I had then to work out from where to start the search..."

Dr. Tamworth was not to be outdone. His quick mind and strong analytical abilities had presented him with the solution before Holmes could elaborate further. "I have it, Holmes! You alluded to it earlier, when you described Ellen Cox's passage through the circular area of lawn in the epicentre of the garden. The source of her affection was the sundial. That was the starting point!"

Holmes acknowledged that he was correct. There was a further round of applause and a series of toasts to the ageing academic who seemed a little overwhelmed by the response. My colleague took the opportunity to retrieve his churchwarden from the mantlepiece and filled the bowl with some strong shag tobacco. When the pipe was lit, he sent a plume of thick grey smoke up into the air above the hearth.

"So, with the retrieval of the cash and this timepiece, your theory proved to be correct," said Inspector Eastland, rallying for a further top-up of his glass.

"Yes. The money was returned to the bank. Rather surprisingly, the directors refused to press charges against the three, being determined to keep the matter from the public gaze. In fact, they seemed content that the investigation had highlighted several security flaws which they could address in protecting the bank from any future intrusions. It was a decision which angered my brother, given the lengths he had gone to in securing the arrest of the two men and arranging for them to be transported back to London.

"Dominic Tuttle eventually returned to France, where he accepted a position as a signwriter for a Parisian carriage maker. Ellen Cox and Frank Chilvers went on to marry and still reside at *Appleton House* with their three young children. They have a thriving business creating bespoke timepieces for wealthy and discerning collectors."

Mrs. Grimble had been moved to tears. "Such a marvellous tale, Mr. Holmes. I would encourage Dr. Watson to set it down on paper one day. I'm sure it will delight the legions of readers across the world who now follow your exploits."

The evening was almost at a close, a clock on the shelf closest to Holmes's bureau announcing that it was ten o'clock with just two hours until Christmas was once again upon us. While Billy and Mrs. Hudson began to clear the table of bottles, glasses, side plates and napkins, we said our farewells, with each guest expressing their appreciation for the food and entertainment which had been provided. Inspector Lestrade was the last to leave, shaking our hands firmly before retrieving his cape and brown Derby from the coat stand and heading off down the stairs. We heard the door bang behind him and sat down to enjoy a final smoke and to reflect on the evening.

"Exhausting," said Holmes.

"Exhilarating," I replied. "You really must let me record the case. I know it will be popular."

"If you must, but there is one final detail you may wish to add. I will, of course, leave that to your discretion as the chronicler of my adventures." He pointed towards the doors of the large oak cabinet which sat to one side of the study. "If you care to look inside there, you will find a Christmas present. But please, take care, it is exceptionally heavy, unbelievably rare, and needs to be handled with the utmost delicacy, for it must be kept upright."

I stepped over to the cabinet and opened both doors. Within the space was a parcel some two feet in height and a foot and a half in width. I turned back to Holmes, who merely laughed at my hesitancy. "Go on, man, open it!"

I peeled back the layers of thick green wrapping paper, being careful not to disturb the item within, although I could already tell that it was rooted firmly to the floor of the cabinet. The unwrapping revealed a most exquisite clock, set with the most beautiful gemstones I had ever seen, and framed within a case constructed of gold, silver, and platinum. The effect was stunning.

"It's a mercury powered timepiece," said Holmes by way of explanation. "The same internal mechanism which was used to open the locking mechanism of the vault. Some months after the conclusion of the case, I was contacted by Ellen Cox, who had by then become Mrs. Ellen Chilvers. She invited me to revisit *Appleton House*, where I was greeted warmly by her and her new husband. They had invited me to their home to give me the clock as a gift. The original workings had been rehoused within the ornate case you now see. While extremely grateful to them, I have never really known what to do with it. In all my time here at Baker Street, the clock has been tucked away at the bottom of a wardrobe. But I will say this, when I retrieved it earlier this week, it had not lost so much as a second in time."

I was struggling to find the words to thank my dear friend, for it was, without doubt, the most lavish gift I had ever received in my life. "This must be worth a small fortune," I exclaimed. "I don't know what to say other than thank you. In the circumstances, I'm afraid you might be a little underwhelmed when you see what I have bought for you!"

We both laughed and I stubbed out what remained of my cigar. "Then you had planned to tell that story tonight well before being invited to by Dr. Tamworth?"

"Yes, it was a small deceit. Having rediscovered the clock, I knew it would be a tale sufficient to entertain our guests for what might otherwise have been a long and very dull evening!"

"Agreed. But there is one point on which I remain unclear."

"And that is...?"

"Why did Mr. and Mrs. Chilvers feel the need to give you such an extraordinary gift? I'm surprised they even invited you to the house, given that it was you who scuppered their intricately planned heist."

"I must admit to being a little dishonest in my earlier retelling of the story. It was not at all surprising that the directors of the bank chose to bring no charges against the three, for that was what I recommended them to do to prevent a public scandal. And it was true that the episode enabled the bank to improve its security arrangements. My actions probably helped the gang to escape prison sentences of between ten and fifteen years. For Ellen and Frank, who had already endured many years of enforced separation, that would have been too much to bear. Her motivation in planning the crime was anger, not greed. Anger that a trusted institution could be so reckless with her family's legacy. The stolen money was returned to the bank. In my view, that was justice restored. To prosecute them beyond that would have been wholly unjust. Sadly, that was not the view shared by my brother. When the bank agreed to my recommendation, Mycroft was furious. It was many months before he would speak to me again."

It had been a memorable evening, and with the gift I had received it was one which I was never to forget. The clock was always given pride of place in all the properties I resided in thereafter. I had only to glance at the delicately balanced hands of that perpetually driven timepiece to be reminded of that special Christmas and my absolute respect and devotion for the man who was Mr. Sherlock Holmes.

Note: *Cox's Timepiece* was an object of curiosity and wonder and had a long history of public display. From 1768 until 1774 it was exhibited in Cox's own museum in Charing Cross, London. By 1796, the clock was on display in Thomas Week's Royal Mechanical Museum in Titchbourne Street, where it remained until 1837. The astronomer James Ferguson once described the timepiece as "the most ingenious piece of mechanism I ever saw in my life." – JHW.

4. The Case of the SS Bokhara

I have mentioned more than once that it was only on a few sporadic occasions that my colleague chose to share with me tantalising details of the many adventures he had experienced during those three years of his self-imposed exile from May 1891. Even when he did refer to one of his exploits, Holmes would often be reluctant to provide any real details of what had transpired. So it came as something of a surprise when he began to talk about the sinking of a steam passenger ship and his near-death experience off the Pescadores islands in the Straight of Formosa in October 1892.

"Are you acquainted with Dr. Lowson?" he asked, that particular morning, as we sat together enjoying coffee and cigars within the spacious lounge of a gentlemen's club in Pall Mall.

I looked up from my medical journal, unaware that Holmes had been looking across at the article I was reading. "Only by reputation – he was, of late, a surgeon with the Hong Kong civil service. A friend of mine in the army medical corps is stationed there and speaks very highly of him. You should read this, it's a fascinating article. Lowson debunks some of the medical myths about drowning, based on his own experience of escaping from a sinking ship[2]."

"Yes, he was lucky to escape the wreck of the *SS Bokhara*. A terrible business."

---

[2] Lowson, James A, *Sensations in Drowning*, Edinburgh Medical Journal, 13 (1), pp 41-45, January 1903.

"Then you have read the article?"

"No, no. I met Lowson at the time, for I was also on board the steamer that day."

I stubbed out what remained of my cigar and looked at him aghast. "You were on board the ship when it sank?"

"Yes, I was working my passage from Shanghai. The ship was carrying a valuable cargo of gold and I had been commissioned to ensure that nothing unexpected happened to it before it could be offloaded in Hong Kong. To my fellow sailors – most of whom were lascars and indentured Chinese deckhands – I was Bill Cartwright, an East End seafarer with an appetite for adventure. In reality, I was working for the Hong Kong and Shanghai Banking Corporation, protecting its consignment of bullion. My brother Mycroft had made the arrangements to keep me from the clutches of what remained of Professor Moriarty's foot soldiers."

It was an astonishing revelation and I was eager to learn more. "Lowson recounts how the vessel ran into a typhoon on the 9th of October and never escaped its clutches."

"That is correct. We set sail on the 8th and were due to arrive in Hong Kong on the 11th. The P&O vessel was carrying 148 people and 150 tons of cargo. The typhoon had not been forecast and hit us hard that first night. It left the ship adrift in the Straits of Formosa. I was below deck, working with others to do what we could to pump out the massive quantities of water which threatened to sink the ship. By the following morning we had lost all the lifeboats and most of the deckhouse. And while we expected the winds to subside, they continued to worsen throughout the day and into the night, until three enormous waves finally overcame the vessel, flooding the engine rooms, and plunging the ship into darkness. The engineers did what they could to try to fix the steam boilers, but it was too late – with land sighted only a few hundred yards downwind, we struck a reef sometime close to midnight. It ripped open the starboard side, scuppering the steamer within minutes."

I could scarcely believe that Holmes had never sought to relay the story and was gripped by the narrative. "How did you survive?" I asked.

"More by luck than judgment, Watson! We were working by the light of tallow dips, when one of the quartermasters came below to tell us to make our way up to the bridge as he feared that the ship would be lost. He brought with him a dozen lifebelts. There seemed to be some confusion, with many of the Asian sailors refusing to don the belts. I had no such compunction and alongside the engineers happily took a belt and headed up to the deck. I would say that most of the passengers and crew had done the same by the time the ship began to slide inexorably beneath the waves. The stewards were doing their best to bark out orders, but most of those around me looked paralysed with fear. I took my chances in the water, jumping off the port side as a wave swept across the deck. It carried me some length from the ship, a distance sufficient to prevent me from being sucked down by the maelstrom. It was difficult to make headway, but the lifebelt kept me afloat and the prevailing winds ensured that I was pushed unerringly in the direction of Sand Island which lay less than 500 yards from the reef. When I was eventually driven onto the shore, I managed to scramble behind a large rock, which gave me a measure of protection. I then spent the rest of the night helping others who had managed to escape the stricken vessel."

"Is that when you met James Lowson?"

"Yes, he was travelling back from a match at the Shanghai Cricket Club. Of the thirteen cricketers on board, only Lowson and a Lieutenant Markham survived the sinking. Lowson was in a pretty poor state, barefoot, still clad in what remained of his pyjamas, and covered in lacerations. With the help of some of the lascar sailors who had found their way on to the beach, we carried him to a ruined hut on the uninhabited island, where he slept fitfully for a few hours."

"Lowson hints at a few adventures after reaching the shore. So what happened next?"

Holmes took a sip from his coffee and placed the cup and saucer on a low table to his side. With a solemn look, he continued: "We had further difficulties. There were about twenty of us by the early hours of the next morning, an assorted mix of officers, passengers, and sailors. The hut provided some shelter, but the rough stone floor made any sort of rest near impossible. The next day we foraged for any washed-up items that might make our accommodation more bearable but were then set upon by a band of marauding fishermen who had travelled across to the island to salvage what they could from the wreckage. As they were carrying axes and knives, we had little option but to comply. However, being able to speak a little Mandarin, I was able to persuade them to take us to one of the inhabited islands nearby. There we were well looked after by the locals who fed us and patched up our wounds as best they could."

A question then occurred to me. "Did you continue to maintain the charade that you were Bill Cartwright?"

He chuckled. "Yes, but it proved to be difficult, for a reason I will come onto. I had by this time struck up an acquaintance with Dr. Lowson. In many respects, he reminded me of you – a quiet, resolute fellow with a genuine concern for others. He was proud of his Scottish roots and steadfastly refused to be browbeaten by anyone around him. I found myself talking to him at some length, all the while fearing that I might be revealing too much of my true self. He was still extremely weak and many of his wounds had become inflamed. So much so, that I spoke to our hosts in the village and arranged for our party to be transported to the city of Ma Gong where I believed we would be better able to recuperate. I had two motives for doing so. Firstly, to assist Lowson and the other survivors, and secondly, to make plans for the recovery of the gold from the *SS Bokhara*."

"I had quite forgot that part of the story!" said I.

"Yes, I too would have forgot about the gold had the ship been swept away or lost to the depths. But I knew her to be lodged within the relatively shallow waters close to the reef, making the recovery of the bullion a possibility. And I had a local contact I knew I could trust to organise such a salvage operation."

I was at once intrigued: "Really? Who was that?"

"The local mandarin of Ma Gong – an influential official I had once met in London some years before. I assisted him in relocating a small stolen statue, a representation of an ancient sea goddess. He could not have been happier. In conversation with some of the locals, I learned that he was still alive and very much in control of the thriving city. Disregarding any threats to my own safety, I arranged for a brief note to be sent, explaining our predicament, and requesting his assistance. Luckily, he was only too pleased to help."

I was surprised to hear that Holmes had taken such an approach. "So you didn't send the note as 'Bill Cartwright'?"

"No. The mandarin generally considered himself to be superior to most foreigners. I feared that an unsolicited request from an unknown English seaman might be ignored, or, at worst, construed as lacking in respect for his position.

By then, some days had passed since the sinking of the ship, and I felt compelled to act for everyone's sake."

"And what was the outcome?"

Holmes beamed. "The official's response was overwhelming and more than a little surreal. We were transported to his palatial home and afforded every luxury. A party was thrown in our honour, attended by local dignitaries. Alongside Lowson, Markham and the officers from the ship, I was treated to a champagne reception. I had asked the mandarin to keep my identity secret, something which he did with admirable tact, explaining only that I had once assisted him when he visited London. This was enough to convince my colleagues, who were incredulous that I could have engineered such an invitation. In their minds, it also helped to explain why I had been able to speak to the locals in their own tongue."

It was my turn to smile. "Then you were able to maintain the masquerade?"

"Indeed. I found time to speak alone with the man. He said he was extremely excited to receive my note, as he had believed me to be dead. I realised then that the news of my demise at the Reichenbach Falls had even reached the faraway islands of the Pescadores! Assuring him that I was very much alive, but still fearful of being pursued by international assassins, I placed myself at his mercy and made my requests. The approach seemed to appeal to his vanity. The following day, he arranged for several official vessels to make their way to the reef where the *SS Bokhara* had been dashed. On board were around a dozen local divers who began to work in pairs, descending to where the vessel lay and painstakingly recovering the small chests of gold that were still housed within the hold of the ship.

"The weather favoured the divers' endeavours, and the sea remained calm throughout the two days it took to conclude the work. I had been reluctant to tell the officers of the ship about the salvage operation but did confide in both Dr. Lowson and Lieutenant Markham in order to put a plan into action. All three of us spent some time on board a sailing junk watching the divers at work. Both men proved invaluable in assisting the locals when any bodies were discovered within the wreck. In short, by the third day, all of the gold had been retrieved and arrangements were made for the bodies to be placed in coffins for the onward passage to Hong Kong."

I ordered fresh coffee from a waiter who entered the lounge at that point. He had clearly heard the closing part of my colleague's narrative and looked at me slightly askance. I tried to reassure him with a gentle nod and a smile. Holmes merely continued with his account.

"There is little to add to the tale beyond that I'm afraid. Through the intervention of the mandarin we were picked up by the *Thales*, a vessel run by the Douglas Steamship Company. From there, we transferred to the torpedo cruiser *HMS Porpoise* which transported all the survivors and the coffins of the dead to the port of Hong Kong. On board, only Lowson, Markham and I knew that some of these caskets contained the recovered gold."

"Very clever, Holmes – and I imagine that your employers at the bank were delighted with the extraordinary efforts you had gone to in maintaining their assets?"

"There was something of a bonus payment, which eventually found its way into the benevolent fund set up for the victims of the *SS Bokhara*. Of course, I lost contact with Lowson, moving on within a few days to travel to Colombo. I regretted that I had not been able to reveal my true identity to him but knew that any such disclosure might place him in further danger beyond all that he had already endured."

I felt I had to interject. "Well, you may feel vindicated by your decision. Only two years later he was to play a lead role in diagnosing the outbreak of the bubonic plague in the Government Civil Hospital in Hong Kong. His work, and that of the other surgeons at the hospital, undoubtedly saved many thousands of lives."

Holmes looked surprised. "I did not know that. Although I still had a few challenges of my own in that year..."

His gaze was fixed upon the mantelpiece and he seemed momentarily to have drifted off into his own recollections. I sought to bring him back: "Well, that was certainly a most remarkable and unexpected tale."

Snapped out of his reverie he gave me a steely look. "Please tell me that you do not plan to write up some romanticised account of this affair. I fear it would make very dull reading. You would do better to transcribe the singular features surrounding my very next adventure, which featured a most extraordinary blowpipe. Beyond Colombo, I became embroiled in an investigation into the murder of a Tibetan priest at the hands of a Genoese merchant. I will relay the pertinent facts when we are back in Baker Street..."

So saying, he finished his coffee, rose quickly from his seat, and gestured towards the door of the lounge. I was never to learn any more about the unfortunate priest, the merchant or, indeed, the blowpipe. When we reached 221B, Holmes received an urgent telegram from Scotland Yard, inviting him to investigate an unusual case of patricide in Walthamstow. He set off immediately and did not return to his consulting room for two days.

I feel I owe it to my dear friend to set down the case of the *SS Bokhara*. While there was no mystery to be uncovered or conundrum to be solved, it helps to fill in another small chapter in that extended period he so often referred to as his "Great Hiatus."

5. The Misadventure of the Norfolk Poacher

One particularly cold morning in the November of 1903 my colleague announced suddenly that he desired a short excursion to the countryside. Such was my surprise at his proclamation that I set down my medical journal and directed my full attention towards him.

"Really, Holmes? Do you have anywhere particular in mind?"

"Somewhere isolated, with a long stretch of coastline. A place where a man can fish in the morning, hunt in the afternoon and shoot in the evening."

I gave him a wry grin. "Then you already have that place in mind?"

"Indeed. I think a couple of days in North Norfolk should do the trick. I trust you will join me?"

"Certainly. But first, you must tell me the real reason you are so keen to trek off into the wilds of East Anglia!"

This time it was he that smiled. "Watson, there is no fooling you. It will be good to escape the capital for a short while and take in some fine country air, but I cannot deny that I have an ulterior motive." He stepped across to the table and retrieved that morning's edition of *The Times*. "Here, cast your eyes over this."

My attention was directed towards a short piece in the left-hand column of the folded broadsheet. It read:

POACHER SHOT DEAD ON BILLINGTON ESTATE

Gamekeeper arrested for murder

The dead body of a sixty-three-year-old man was found in the early hours of yesterday morning in a clearing close to woods on the Billington Estate near Holt. A police spokesman said that the man had been shot and had sustained injuries to the head, chest, and upper legs. Early enquiries suggest that the deceased was Joe Whistlethorpe, a local poacher well-known to estate workers. It is believed that he had ventured onto the estate the previous evening in pursuit of gamebirds.

The Norfolk County Constabulary has revealed no further details at this time, but did confirm that Toby Baxter, an assistant gamekeeper on the estate, has been arrested in connection with the shooting.

I passed the paper back to Holmes who was then in the process of lighting a briar pipe. "Why are you so eager to travel up to Holt for such a parochial affair?" I asked, somewhat bewildered.

"A fair challenge, my friend. And the short answer is that I have a particular and personal interest. You see Toby Baxter was, until nine months ago, a stalwart member of the Baker Street Irregulars, a loyal and dedicated foot soldier. When he mentioned to me that he had seen an advertisement for the assistant gamekeeper's position – and fancied a return to the county of his birth – I urged him to apply and agreed to write him a reference. I had little doubt that his diverse range of talents and resourcefulness would serve him well in the role but guessed that he might be viewed with some suspicion by the head gamekeeper, having little by way of direct experience."

"In other words, you addressed your reference to Sir Terence Billington, who happens to be a fellow member of the Savile Club and the man you once assisted in *The Case of the Diligent Philanthropist*."

"You have it in one, Watson! Baxter was taken on and had, to this point, proved himself to be a reliable and trustworthy employee."

"But if the trip is designed to assist Baxter, how can you be sure that he isn't guilty of the murder?"

"Well, that remains to be seen. The invitation to assist didn't come from Baxter, but from Sir Terence, who sent me a telegram late last night. He is the local magistrate and is treading very carefully given that the young estate worker is his employee. He asked the Chief Constable of Norfolk if I might be permitted to work with his officers in the early part of the investigation. As no objections were raised, I am to travel up to North Norfolk on the Midland and Great Northern line a little later. And despite the wishes of the coroner, the Chief Constable has also been persuaded to keep the body where it is for the moment, so that I may see it at the scene. A ten-thirty departure from King's Cross should see us there by the early afternoon."

"Do you think Sir Terence believes him to be guilty?"

"Not a bit of it. He is unconvinced but has to be seen to be acting impartially."

"And the police?"

"Again, they are acting as they have to, but have been compelled to arrest Baxter."

"For what reason?"

Holmes paused briefly and inhaled on the briar: "Because he has confessed to the shooting."

****

Holmes was in a lively mood as we travelled up to Holt on the picturesque rural line, taking advantage of a quiet corner in the train's dining car. It had been some time since we had spent such a long journey together and I was reminded of just how entertaining Holmes could be when rejuvenated by a case. His talk was of crime in the rural shires and the deep-rooted culture of poaching in counties like Norfolk – where many country-dwellers were still driven to take game as an economic necessity and small bands of professional poachers could make a tidy living selling birds they pilfered from the landed estates. It was ever thus.

It was a little after two-thirty that afternoon when we finally arrived at the Billington Estate. The skies were already beginning to darken and there was a distinct nip in the air. As we climbed down from the small trap we had hired at the railway station, a tall lean man with a full greying beard came out of the hall to greet us. Sir Terence was effusive in greeting Holmes and shook my hand vigorously as I was introduced to him.

"It is a pleasure to meet you, Dr Watson! I feel that I know you already given the many times Holmes has told me stories of your derring-do and inestimable talents as a surgeon."

I felt a twinge of embarrassment as he said this; somewhat surprised to learn that I had been the subject of any conversation within the cloistered interior of the Savile Club.

Holmes had clearly noted my discomfort and gave me a sly wink.

We spent but a short time at Billington Hall. Sir Terence arranged for some cold meat sandwiches to be brought into the library and insisted that we take a pot of tea with him. We sat before a large bay window overlooking the rose garden of the estate. While neither Holmes nor I were particularly hungry, we accepted his kind invitation. Our host seemed content to talk while the two of us ate and drank.

"Your man Baxter has been as good as gold since joining my staff, Holmes. Isaac Aldous, the head gamekeeper, has been particularly impressed by him. He now has a comprehensive knowledge of the area and has quickly familiarised himself with all the tenant farmers and tradesmen who serve the estate. He is well-liked by most of those who have come into contact with him but has been resolute in seeing off some of the more unsavoury characters who venture onto my lands without permission."

"Is the local poaching fraternity such a big concern?" asked Holmes, placing his empty plate down beside him.

Sir Terence smiled. "Am I detecting just a hint of sympathy for those that might be persuaded to steal game that does not belong to them...?

Holmes answered him directly. "Not at all, but I am keen to know whether the taking of birds from the estate is generally perpetrated by opportunists – keen to add some fresh meat to their meagre diet – or a more determined breed of professional poachers who profit from their illicit trade."

Our host nodded. "I can understand why you draw the distinction, but as a magistrate I am bound to say that the law does not favour one above the other. Like most enlightened landowners, I do not wish to see a return to the dark days of the *game laws* when men could be hanged or transported for merely being caught in possession of a snare or firearm with intent to poach. But if I were to allow the many impoverished farm folk that live in the villages encircling this estate to wander onto my lands any time they wished in order to fill their pots, chaos would ensue, and the very fabric of our social structure would be undermined. Fortunately, as far as I am aware, the only problems we have are with a small, but determined, cohort of poachers that reside mainly on the western fringe of the estate in the village of Letheringsett."

My colleague was unfazed by the admonition. "Is that where Joe Whistlethorpe lived?"

"Yes – a frequent offender well-known to the bench. His list of poaching offences stretches back over forty years."

"And was he given to violence in carrying out his work?"

"Yes, indeed. On the rare occasions he was confronted on this estate, he was quite content to use his fists or a wooden cudgel to evade capture. On one occasion he threatened an assistant gamekeeper with a shotgun, although no charge was brought against him as he readily accepted the lesser charge of poaching."

Holmes seemed keen to curtail our discussions, no doubt eager to reach the body while there was still some light. He had one further question: "Sir Terence, in the telegram you sent me last night, you were adamant that Baxter is innocent. Have you been to see the body yourself?"

It struck me as an odd question to put to our host, but Sir Terence seemed unperturbed. "No, Mr. Aldous furnished me with all of the relevant facts. Toby Baxter took him to see the body at about eight o'clock yesterday morning."

Holmes smirked enigmatically. "Then we will trouble you no further, Sir Terence. I thank you for your hospitality but think we should get out to see the body ourselves while there is still a glimmer of daylight."

Sir Terence stood promptly and directed an arm towards the door of the library. "As you wish. I have arranged for Mr. Aldous to walk you out to the clearing. It is perhaps a mile all told, in an area known as the Crinkle Crankle Plantation. If you follow me, I will take you to him."

Isaac Aldous was a stout, ruddy-faced man with enormous side whiskers. He retained a good head of dark hair and had intense green eyes. Clad in a well-worn tweed jacket, flat cap, waistcoat and plus fours, he was every bit the Norfolk gamekeeper. Sir Terence left us in his charge and we at once set off along a muddy track towards a fringe of woodland that ran along the western flank of the estate. Aldous proved to be good company, happy to answer any questions put to him and taking time to explain the layout of the estate and any features he thought relevant.

It was some minutes into our trek before Holmes was minded to enquire about the discovery of the body. "Tell me, Mr. Aldous. Did you not think it odd that Baxter should rouse you from your bed on Wednesday and take you to the body? If he were the killer, would it not seem more likely that he should have sought to hide the body or otherwise claim ignorance of the shooting?"

Aldous gave him a broad grin and a knowing nod. "Yes, Sir – that thought was to occur to me a little later in the day. But let me explain what happened. Baxter had been doing the night shift. Ordinarily, I have two men on the rota, but that evening one of the other keepers had been laid low with a severe case of the shingles. Yesterday morning, Baxter came a-hammering on the door of my cottage in something of a panic. I dressed quickly as he explained that he had found Whistlethorpe's body on the plantation. He said he knew someone had been out poaching and had gone to investigate. He found that Whistlethorpe had been shot dead."

"So, no admission at that point?"

"No. We left the cottage and I followed him to where the body lay. It was Whistlethorpe all right, and he was as dead as a door nail, his 12-bore shotgun lying beside him, the breech open. I told Baxter to be careful where he walked, because I knew the police would want to examine the scene for footprints and other evidence."

Holmes interjected. "Did you approach the body from the same direction that Baxter had, in finding the body earlier?"

"Yes, Mr. Holmes. It was along this very path. You will see when we get there in a few moments. The body lay on its back, and we approached the head end first, if that makes sense?"

"Perfectly, my good fellow. And were you inclined to believe all that Baxter had said to that point?"

Aldous nodded definitively. "I had every reason to do so. I have always found him to be honest and forthright and have a great deal of affection for him. And as we walked towards the body I could see the earlier marks of his boots in the mud ahead of us, running to the right of the track. On the left, the prints ran in the opposite direction. As a gamekeeper, I pay particular attention to animal tracks and footprints. They tell me a great deal. And I recognised Baxter's distinct boot print."

Holmes could barely conceal his delight. "Splendid! Note that, Watson – a man who both sees *and* observes. Now, this boot print, what was so distinctive about it?"

"All of the workers on this estate are provided with two pairs of boots each year as part of their employment. We buy them from a bootmaker in Holt who gives us a good price, given the size of our order. When Baxter joined us he was issued with a pair but could not get on with them. He has a particularly broad foot and is pigeon-toed. He said he found the boots to be uncomfortable. In the end, he bought two pairs of hob-nailed boots from a shop in Sheringham."

"Yes, as you say, the pattern is quite distinctive." Holmes had stopped suddenly and now knelt on the track examining the ground with a silver-framed magnifying glass. There was a hint of irritation in his voice. "That is despite the footfall of what looks like an army of police boots. Let us hope that the crime scene has been better preserved. Now, you were telling us what happened when you reached the body, Mr. Aldous. Pray continue..."

"Well, I knelt down to check if there were any signs of life. I have never liked Whistlethorpe but would not have wished that upon him. You will see what I mean when we get there. Anyway, as I did so, I saw a small grey object lying ahead of the body, perhaps fifteen feet away to my left, and at the edge of the woods. Baxter had continued to stand behind me, and when I pointed towards the object and then looked towards him, he began to sob. Some seconds later, he admitted that it was he who had shot the poacher. From then on, he refused to say anything further until the police arrived."

"That is curious," said I, "and what was this grey object?"

"A sealskin cap – although I did not know that until a little later when the police had concluded their search. Having confirmed that Whistlethorpe was dead, I led Baxter back to my cottage, took his shotgun and sat him down in the kitchen. My wife sat with him while I ran up to the hall to ask one of the servants to contact the police. When the police arrived, I explained what had been said and Baxter was arrested and later taken into custody. They also retained his shotgun. You can probably see the police officers up ahead now, gentlemen. That is where the body is. I'm sure they will be happy to tell you what they have discovered so far."

We had reached the clearing in the woods and as we approached the body we could see two policemen standing guard. At various points across the plantation I could see small stakes driven into the ground, some with string attached, others topped with what looked like ticker tape. A tall, uniformed officer stepped forward to greet us, nodding and smiling at Aldous, and extending a hand towards Holmes who still held before him the tell-tale magnifying glass. "Delighted to meet you, sir. I am Chief Inspector Ellis of the Holt Police..." He beckoned towards his fellow officer, "...and this is Police Constable Peck."

Holmes smiled benignly, already looking beyond the two officers at the corpse some ten feet away and the web of stakes and string radiating from it. "It is a pleasure to meet you both. This is my colleague, Doctor Watson."

With the pleasantries completed, Holmes asked only to be left alone to survey the scene and started with a close examination of the body. The sallow-skinned chief inspector seemed perfectly content with this, explaining that they had already concluded their search and had gathered all the available evidence. He confirmed furthermore that he had been told by the chief constable to allow Holmes complete discretion to conduct an independent evaluation. So it was that the four of us headed towards a makeshift canvas shelter that had been erected nearby. Chatting and smoking, we watched as Holmes spent the next thirty minutes moving hither and thither across the plantation, occasionally disappearing from view – pacing and squatting, kneeling, and retrieving – until the very last shafts of light had departed from the pink-hued sky and we were plunged suddenly into darkness.

With some lanterns lit under the canvas, Holmes joined our group and accepted the offer of a cigarette. He went immediately to the back of the shelter where a trestle table had been set up. On top of this were laid out several wooden trays and a shotgun, which I imagined to be the weapon the police had seized from Toby Baxter. He began immediately to sift through the contents of the trays and spent some time looking over the shotgun.

"Very thorough, Chief Inspector," said Holmes, looking back momentarily before continuing his examination. "This represents all of the findings from your search, the original location of each being marked by the stakes and the handwritten labels you have positioned across the plantation."

It was more of a statement than a question and prompted but a weary, "Yes, sir".

Chief Inspector Ellis seemed uncomfortable with the silence that followed: "So, Mr. Holmes – I think you will agree that this is a pretty open and shut case? Having concluded our work, we now have enough evidence to charge Toby Baxter with murder."

Aldous coughed unexpectedly, rocked slightly and looked momentarily stunned at the disclosure. Holmes laid a comforting arm on his sleeve and smiled at the gamekeeper as if to reassure him. He then addressed the chief inspector. "You have no doubt noted the very distinct footprints that lead along this track to the head of the body. Mr. Aldous here will have confirmed to you that these are Toby Baxter's. He will also have told you that the same footprints can be seen running in the opposite direction. This confirms that Baxter did, at some point earlier, approach the head of the body – most likely to confirm the identity and death of the poacher – before heading back to the estate to rouse Mr. Aldous from his bed. While less clear, we can see the tangible evidence that he made the return trip accompanied by Mr. Aldous. Their fresh tracks can be picked out occasionally, although most have been obscured by the heavy footfall of others who have visited the scene subsequently..."

Ellis was clearly in no mood to be rebuked on his own turf and cut in quickly: "Now, steady on, Mr. Holmes. We've done a thorough job and had no option but to cut across some of the tracks in reaching the body. You will have noted that our searches beyond that point have been conducted along a few well-marked lines, so as not to compromise the scene."

Holmes responded enthusiastically. "Chief Inspector – rest assured, I have nothing but admiration for the way that you have carried out your work. I have rarely seen a better police search, and the very scientific way that you have mapped out your findings is an approach I would commend other forces to adopt. As for the evidence, there is no doubt that we can place Baxter at the scene. But why do you believe he killed Whistlethorpe?"

Ellis frowned. "I'd have thought that was obvious if you'd noted the footprints beyond the body – the ones that run over there, from the crinkle-crankle wall to that large oak tree at the edge of the woods. That is where the killer stood, in hiding. He watched Whistlethorpe emerge from the trees and walk out into the plantation. When the poacher turned to look back towards the woods, our man seized the opportunity and shot him at close range. The footprints confirm all of that. I would suggest that the shooter called to Whistlethorpe to make him turn around."

"Possibly," mused Holmes, "that is certainly possible. Now, let me be clear about the evidence as you see it. You will not mind if I throw in a few polite challenges along the way?"

While his expression confirmed exactly what the officer thought of the proposition, Ellis responded in the affirmative.

"We start at the boundary of the estate. Our killer scales the wall and drops down on to the plantation. I see it as no coincidence that he should pick that spot, as the overhanging branch from the elm tree allows for a straightforward climb down, while the crumbling brickwork on the inside means that the return journey is also likely to be straightforward. The footprints at the base of the wall confirm both the entry and exit. We then have two sets of footprints. One runs from the wall to the oak tree. The other gives us evidence of the return journey."

"Exactly as I told you, Mr. Holmes. And the fact that he waited by the oak tree for some time is indicated by the two cigarette butts we recovered from the spot. Furthermore, I would suggest that this also gives us confirmation of premeditation."

"Agreed. I have no issue with any of that. My initial challenge is why Baxter would scale a wall twice when he lives and works on the estate and is free to go about as he chooses."

"Perhaps he had been following the poacher outside of the estate and this was the quickest route to where he knew the offender was heading."

Holmes looked unconvinced but carried out. "Let us then turn to Mr. Whistlethorpe himself. His passage through the woods is clear and as an experienced poacher he is most likely to have tried to remain hidden wherever possible. Why then would he have ventured out into the clearing and risk detection on a cloudless and moonlit night?"

PC Peck, who had, to this point, said very little, sniggered. Holmes rounded on him instantly. "You have something constructive to offer at this point, Constable?"

The young fair-haired officer held his ground. "He was pursuing pheasants. They don't always stay in the woods."

"Ah, ha! The young fellow suggests that the poacher may have broken cover in order to bag a gamebird. What say you, Chief Inspector?"

Ellis looked embarrassed at the officer's outburst and gave a straight answer. "We could find no evidence that he had shot at any pheasants before being killed."

Relishing the performance, it was Holmes's turn to break rank. "I would beg to differ, my friend." He pulled from his pocket a small shotgun cartridge, some three or four inches in length. "I retrieved this from just inside the woods. Clear evidence that Whistlethorpe discharged his weapon at least once before being shot himself."

I interjected: "Do you think he took a shot at his attacker?"

Holmes shook his head. "No, the breech of his gun was open. He did that while still in the woods in order to eject the cartridge. PC Peck was not wrong. He shot at a pheasant and then walked out of the woods to retrieve it."

Chief Inspector Ellis was having none of it. "Where's the evidence for that? We found no bird. Are you about to tell me that you have one secreted inside your Inverness cape?"

It was a comment that brought a smile from us all, including Holmes. He responded with admirable aplomb. "If you had moved the body you would have found a small cluster of feathers on the ground." He held one up between his thumb and forefinger. "Now, the real question is what happened to the pheasant?"

Ellis was not to be outdone. "The bird may have been winged and flew off some distance further. Perhaps it was taken by a fox or hen harrier. Who knows? Who cares? You cannot escape the fact that Whistlethorpe was shot at close range by Baxter. The bore of the gun he was carrying matches that of the cartridge retrieved from beneath the oak tree. And as you have already confirmed, the tracks of his hob-nailed boots are visible to and from the wall. It's an open and shut case as I said before."

"Whistlethorpe was shot at close range. That much is true. The spread of the shot is clustered mainly around his chest and lower abdomen. He faced his attacker and saw what was coming, unable to defend himself."

Aldous took a deep breath. "You might call it intuition, but in truth I refuse to believe that Baxter would have chosen to shoot an unarmed man face on, and at close quarters. He had no need to kill him."

Holmes nodded. "I agree. But let me first address the evidence of the shotgun cartridge and footprints. While the cartridge retrieved from beneath the oak tree is indeed the same bore as that used by Baxter, it was not fired from his gun. The cartridge was struck by a blunt firing pin. Baxter's Belgian-manufactured weapon does not have a blunt striker."

Chief Inspector Ellis looked on in disbelief as Holmes continued. "As for the boot prints, they are remarkably similar to Baxter's, being of the self-same pattern and design, but are not identical. I have conducted a very close examination. We are all agreed that the prints which run to the head of the body are those of Baxter himself. The sole of the right boot is particularly distinctive. One of the hob nails is missing from the sole and its absence can be seen clearly in every print deposited in the mud. Try as I might, I can find no comparable print in the tracks between the oak tree and boundary wall. Mr. Aldous also told me earlier that Baxter is pigeon-toed. There is clear evidence of this gait in the prints we know to be Baxter's, but no suggestion of it on the other side of the clearing."

In desperation, the senior officer offered up one final challenge. "What about the sealskin cap, Mr. Holmes? It was also found close to the oak tree and most likely dropped by the killer in his haste to escape. In his statement, Mr. Aldous told us that it was only when he pointed towards the cap that Baxter broke down and confessed to the shooting. What explanation could there be, other than the fact that the cap belonged to Baxter and he feared it to be a clue which would tie him to this foul deed?"

Aldous was quick to defend his colleague. "Sir, I am bound to say that I have never seen Baxter wearing such a cap."

It was a telling blow and Ellis looked visibly deflated. Holmes carried on. "There are some very distinct clues which I would like to pursue now, gentleman. I am sure that you will be much relieved, Chief Inspector, in being free to release the body into the capable hands of the police surgeon and coroner. I would of course be interested in any fresh facts which emerge from the *post mortem*. Now, Mr. Aldous, I would be grateful if you could lead us back to Billington Hall."

"Certainly, Mr. Holmes. Sir Terence is expecting you. I understand he has arranged rooms for you both within the hall itself."

Holmes nodded but surprised us all with his response. "That is most kind, but I am afraid that we must decline the offer. I will of course explain my reasons to Sir Terence when we arrive back at the hall and retrieve our overnight bags. I have in mind to stay at one of your local hostelries. I am sure that you can suggest one that offers the very best in hot cooked meals. All this talk of gamebirds has left me with quite an appetite. Is there a good local inn that routinely serves roast pheasant?"

Isaac Aldous was only too pleased to provide him with an answer. "I can suggest the very place. You will need to venture no further than the *King's Head* at Letheringsett. There is no inn to match it for miles around."

****

When we arrived back at the hall, my colleague spent some time briefing Sir Terence on what he had discovered. I retrieved our bags from the hallway and waited for him in the lounge. When he returned, Holmes informed me that our very gracious host had arranged for his four-wheeler to transport us the two miles to the *King's Head.*

We arrived at the inn a few minutes before six o'clock. Our rooms were small, but tidy, and perfectly adequate for our short stopover. Having freshened up, we made our way downstairs into the taproom and ordered a pint each of local ale and enquired about the food that evening. To Holmes's delight, the landlady confirmed that pheasant was indeed on the menu. A short while later we were sat at a large oak table tucking in to a splendid roast meal.

I took the opportunity to quiz him: "Why did you not want to stay at the hall?"

He took a sip from his beer glass and lowered his voice. "Murky affairs, Watson. This is a complex affair which will take some unravelling. I suspect that some of the vital information we need lies outside of the estate and in this very village. Let us think back to the nature of this crime. Our killer lies in wait, and then watches Whistlethorpe as he shoots a pheasant and goes to retrieve it. With the victim unable to defend himself, our killer strikes. Having committed the act, he does not leave in haste – dropping the cap as the chief inspector would have us believe – but chooses to walk across to the body and pick up the dead bird. Why would he do that?"

"Perhaps he was hungry."

"Possibly, but I suspect his motivation is more entrenched than that. I would venture that he's used to stealing gamebirds."

"Ah ha! Then you believe he may also be a poacher?"

"It would fit with the clues we have. Whistlethorpe was a seasoned felon. It would not be an easy task to track him as he sought out his prey. He would be alert to every sight and sound as he made his way through that woodland. So, who better to pursue him than a fellow poacher – one who also knew the geography of the estate and where the man was heading. We know that Whistlethorpe lived in Letheringsett. It does not take a great leap of faith to imagine that his killer lived close by and knew him. That should narrow our list of suspects."

He finished his ale and placed the glass down beside his empty dinner plate. "That was a fine meal, my friend. So much so, that I think I will make a particular point of thanking the landlady and praising her culinary skills. I will be back in a few minutes."

I suspected some subterfuge on his part. When he returned to the table a short while later, I could see that I was not wrong. He had a pronounced grin on his face.

"Come on. I know you well enough to recognise chicanery when I see it. As well as flattering that poor woman for her excellent cooking, I imagine you've been persuading her – albeit softly – to reveal the names of all the local poachers who occasionally arrive at the back door of the inn offering her a ready supply of choice gamebirds. Am I correct?"

"Capital, Watson! A very promising line of enquiry it proved to be. I gave Mrs. Flowerday a small financial incentive and the assurance that anything she revealed to me would not be traced back to her. In return, she has provided me with the names of three local men who all have some form as purveyors of stolen meat. Their names are Stephen Matlock, William Kendrick and – most notably – *Ethan Baxter*."

"A relative of young Toby?!"

"His father, no less. I knew that he lived in the area, for this is where Toby grew up. I also understood him to be estranged from his son. The connection cannot be a coincidence. Either way, we will enjoy an early night and set out first thing tomorrow to discover what we can." So saying, he pushed his chair back from the table, stood up and headed towards the narrow staircase of the inn. "Good night, Watson."

After a solid night's sleep, I arose early the next morning and having washed and shaved, made my way to the taproom for breakfast. Holmes was already sitting at the table, reading a copy of the *Norfolk Chronicle,* and sipping at a cup of steaming black coffee. In the fireplace, there was already a roaring log fire. Mrs. Flowerday was as friendly as she had been the previous night and presented us with two sizeable oval plates on which sat the largest cooked breakfast I had ever seen. Neither of us had any complaints.

We set off from the inn at eight-thirty, heading towards a cottage on the Cley Road which we had been told was the home of Stephen Matlock. Our door knocking prompted some fierce barking from the property adjacent to it. In due course, a short elderly man with a severely twisted spine emerged from the property. He told the dog to pipe down and asked us our business. There was no warmth in his tone, suggesting that he was not unused to being roused by visitors seeking out his neighbour. Holmes attempted to placate the man with some gentle bonhomie, but in the end was compelled to come clean and admit that we wanted to speak to his neighbour about stolen gamebirds. The wizened old fellow laughed on hearing this and said we were wasting our time. Matlock had apparently been arrested three days earlier for a violent assault on a man in Kelling. He was still being held in a local lock-up.

Holmes took him at his word and thanked the man for his help. As we walked away, he said we would need to verify the information but had no doubt that the old man had been telling the truth. That being the case, we now had a suspect list of just two.

William Kendrick proved to be more difficult to locate, and of the three or four locals we met who claimed to know of him, none could provide an address. However, a few discreet enquiries at the post office counter within the local grocery store proved more fruitful. We were told that he had moved into a house on Hurdle Lane, a property rented by none other than Ethan Baxter.

It was Kendrick who answered when we first knocked on the dark green door at the front of the small, two-storey property. He was around five feet, seven inches tall, with an asymmetric face. It was difficult to discern initially whether this was a congenital deformity or the result of some accident that had befallen him earlier in life. But noting the many scars, bumps and bruises that adorned his skull and hands, I was inclined towards the latter. His bloodshot left eye sat much lower than its counterpart and his nose was distinctly off-centre. And with rough grey stubble adorning much of his craggy face and neck he could not claim to be the most debonair of men. In age, I judged him to be a little over sixty.

Kendrick was surprisingly warm in his reception of us. Holmes explained that he was a private detective assisting the police with the investigation into the death of the poacher, Joe Whistlethorpe. Understanding from good sources that Kendrick and Ethan Baxter may have known the dead man, he was keen to find out whether either man could shed any light on the circumstances surrounding the shooting. Kendrick announced that Baxter was not at home, but said he would assist if he could. Beckoning us into the house, he invited us to take a seat within the small living room of the property and asked if we would like a cup of tea.

The room was well-furnished and surprisingly neat. A comfortable green sofa sat against one wall to the left of the fireplace, with two matching armchairs positioned to the right of the hearth. Hanging from the picture rails around the room were country prints displaying various hunting and fishing scenes, and a glass-fronted cabinet in one corner contained a fair collection of china – each piece again adorned with colourful country motifs. When Kendrick returned from the kitchen with a tea tray, the scene could not have been more genteel.

"So you are a poacher, then, Mr. Kendrick?" said Holmes, taking the tea cup that was passed across to him. "And how is business these days?"

Kendrick regarded him with the grimace of a smile. "Now, Mr. Holmes, is that an attempt to be polite or are you asking me that in some sort of official capacity? You must know that when Ethan and I are asked that question by the police, we usually point out that we earn a reasonable living working in a local grain store." For the first time I detected the hint of a soft West Country accent.

Holmes laughed in response. "My dear fellow, please be clear. I am interested only in the facts pertaining to the murder of Joe Whistlethorpe. Let me be a little more direct. Were you, or Mr. Baxter, out poaching on Tuesday night?"

Kendrick answered him affably enough. "No, sir. I spent the evening here, mending some old fishing nets. I cannot vouch for Ethan, though. He went out with his shotgun at about eight forty-five and didn't return until after I'd gone to bed. I don't know what he got up to as I haven't spoken to him. In fact, I haven't seen him since that time."

I expressed some confusion. "Then how do you know he returned at all?"

"Later that night I heard him shuffling about near the back door and the key being turned in the lock. My bedroom is at the back of the house. I can't tell you the precise time, but it must have been well after midnight. I assumed he'd returned – when I came down early yesterday morning, I saw he'd left his muddy boots near the back door and found a plump pheasant hanging on a hook inside the pantry. But when I went to wake him about nine o'clock, found he was not in his room. And he still hasn't returned."

Holmes was staring intently at the man. He then asked, "Does he often disappear without telling you?"

Kendrick's response was not what I expected. "Yes, frequently. I've been living here for three months and we lead very separate lives. He wanted it that way. Didn't want me treading on his toes, poaching-wise. We agreed about our respective patches and we've stuck to them. He said that the less we knew of each other's work, the better. That way we couldn't incriminate each other if one of us was caught. And as a rule, we take it in turns to poach, so one of us can always provide the other with an alibi. In recent weeks, Ethan has been spending more and more time away from home. He led me to believe he had a new lady friend in Sheringham. My guess is he's gone to visit her."

"I see. And when did you first learn of Whistlethorpe's death?"

"Yesterday evening. I went to the *King's Head* for a pint or two and it was the talk of the village. Not that many will shed a tear for Whistlethorpe. He was not a popular man."

"How well did you know him?"

"As well as any – our paths crossed occasionally if you get my meaning. He and Ethan hated each other."

Holmes placed his tea cup back down on the tray and stood up. "That is most interesting, Mr. Kendrick. Now, would you be kind enough to show me the boots that you say Ethan was wearing on Tuesday night and the pheasant in the pantry?"

Kendrick was comfortable to comply with the request and led us out into the hallway of the property and along to a reasonably sized kitchen at the back of the house. Holmes spent some time walking around the room surveying every detail. In addition to a Belfast pot sink and draining board – which sat before a small window on the far wall – the room housed a sizeable Welsh dresser, an oak table and four well-crafted wooden chairs. The back door of the property was positioned to the right of the sink. On the floor, just inside the doorway, we could see the pair of boots that Kendrick had referred to.

Holmes removed a large paper bag from an inside pocket of his cape and placed it on the oak table. He then retrieved the boots from the floor, picking them up carefully by their laces and placing them down gently on the flattened paper. With his magnifying glass to hand, he set about his task, much to the bemusement of Kendrick, who watched in silence for the full five minutes it took. When the detective had finished, he merely looked up, smiled at Kendrick, and announced that he would need to take the boots away. He then moved towards a door on the left wall of the kitchen which housed the pantry.

Kendrick and I took a few steps towards the pantry ourselves, but did not attempt to impede Holmes in his work. When the door was opened, I could see that the room was no more than six or seven feet in length and some four feet wide. On the floor were several baskets containing vegetables, and visible to me were the heads of three fresh cabbages, some leeks, and a sizeable pile of potatoes. While the space contained no window, I could see a small metal grate built into the top of the side wall which provided for a flow of air into the cold storage area. Half way up this wall, and running for the length of the pantry, was a concrete shelf – perhaps eight inches wide – on which sat a variety of jars, jugs, demijohns, and storage containers. In addition to the vegetables, I imagined this to be the full extent of the men's larder.

Holmes looked quickly over the contents of the pantry, turned, and then fixed his gaze on the pheasant which was hanging from a hook just inside the door on the right. To this point, I had not noticed the bird, as my view had been partially obscured. The magnifying glass reappeared, and Holmes spent a few seconds examining the pheasant before announcing that it too would need to be bagged up and taken away. Kendrick voiced no objection and merely nodded his consent.

Content that he had seen everything in the pantry he needed to, Holmes then swung towards Kendrick with a quizzical look. "Where does Mr. Baxter store his shotguns?"

Kendrick pointed towards the door of the kitchen. "We have a small cupboard down the hallway just under the stairs, which we always keep locked. Ethan has only the one shotgun, as do I. They are kept there, along with our store of cartridges.

The poacher led the way and when we reached the cupboard he retrieved a long iron key from his trouser pocket and quickly unlocked the narrow wooden door. He then stepped back to allow Holmes to see inside the small space.

"I take it that the double-barrelled weapon is yours?" said Holmes without turning.

"Yes, Ethan's is the one furthest from you. The 410 gauge."

Holmes took a handkerchief from his pocket and reached in to retrieve the gun. Clasping the barrel with the handkerchief, he brought the weapon into view. When it was clear of the cupboard door, he set the stock down on the floor and knelt close to it, once more making good use of his lens. Somewhat gingerly, he then opened the breech of the gun and directed his attention towards the firing pin and barrel, before closing it once more.

"I'm afraid I will also need to seize this weapon," said Holmes.

"Really?" replied Kendrick. "Then you must believe it had something to do with the shooting."

"I have no doubt that this is indeed the weapon that killed Joe Whistlethorpe," said my friend, lifting the gun once more and walking off with it in the direction of the kitchen.

I had to express some surprise. "So, Ethan Baxter is our man! Let me ask you, Mr. Kendrick, does your friend usually wear any sort of hat when out poaching."

His response was very enlightening. "Yes, he has a waterproof sealskin cap. Never leaves home without it."

I looked towards Holmes who was now returning from the kitchen. His raised eyebrows suggested that he had registered the disclosure, but he interjected somewhat brusquely: "Would it be possible to see outside, to the rear of the property?"

For the first time since our arrival, Kendrick looked surprised. "Eh, certainly, although there's little to see other than a wooden shed and our veg patch."

"I would be very much obliged to you," said Holmes, wasting no time in heading towards the back door. Without waiting, he opened it and strode out into the garden. Kendrick followed close behind.

I was a little bewildered by my colleague's action but knowing his methods did not voice any concern. Kendrick and I stood back as he moved first towards the garden shed, a small six by four-foot wooden structure with one small side window. From there he proceeded down the garden path and spent some time looking over the aforementioned vegetable patch. It was clear that most of the season's crops had already been harvested for a sizeable area of the soil lay bare, having been recently dug over. That said, there were still plenty of winter greens, parsnips, and leeks on display closer to the house.

After only a few minutes, Holmes came back down the path and announced that he had seen all he needed to. He then added, "I have one final request, Mr. Kendrick. I would be grateful if you could accompany the two of us to Billington Hall, where the police will still have a presence. I am sure that they will be keen to take a statement from you on all that you know and take charge of the boots, shotgun and pheasant I plan to present to them."

Kendrick looked unperturbed. "Certainly, Mr. Holmes, but no mention of my occasional night-time activities, eh?"

The detective regarded him keenly. "Sir Terence Billington is the local magistrate examining the case. Are you not already known to him?"

"No, sir. I've only been in this area for a few months. I've never been caught poaching in these parts."

"I see," was all that my friend could add.

The three of us walked the short distance back to the *King's Head*. Holmes had wrapped the shotgun, boots and pheasant in some sacking which Kendrick had kindly provided. It was just as well, for as we approached the inn the sky darkened and a light flurry of sleet began to fall driven by an icy-cold northerly wind. When we entered the taproom, Mrs. Flowerday greeted us kindly and set about preparing some warm sausage rolls, saying that we looked both frozen and famished. While Kendrick and I ate and warmed ourselves by the fire, Holmes left us without explanation, returning half an hour later and announcing that he had sent a telegram to Sir Terence to ask if the four-wheeler could be despatched to collect us.

The carriage pulled up at the inn a few minutes beyond eleven-thirty. We thanked Mrs. Flowerday for her hospitality and I noticed that Holmes added a handsome tip in settling the bill. Ten minutes later we were heading along the long drive towards Billington Hall. PC Peck and another uniformed constable stood awaiting our arrival and when we climbed down from the carriage, Peck took charge of the items that Holmes had wrapped in the sacking, while the other officer gently shepherded Kendrick away to take a statement from him.

Since our departure the day before, Sir Terence had allowed the police to transfer their findings from the scene of the crime to a small box room near the library. Alongside the items taken from the clearing, the police now had numerous photographs showing the position of the body and the various footprints we had seen earlier. Holmes was quick to praise the efforts of the officers in recording everything but gave the images only a passing glance. No sooner had I taken a seat, when he announced that he had one further errand to run and would be back within a couple of hours to explain how and why the murder had occurred. PC Peck looked as bewildered as I, as Holmes headed off without further explanation. It was obviously a pre-arranged excursion, for the four-wheeler had continued to wait at the entrance to the hall to transport him to this new destination.

****

It was nearly three hours later when Holmes finally returned to Billington. Already assembled in the library were Sir

Terence and Isaac Aldous, alongside myself, William Kendrick and the two local constables. When my colleague entered the room he was accompanied by Chief Inspector Ellis and a dejected-looking man I did not recognise.

"Gentlemen, you must forgive me!" said Holmes with some gusto. "It has taken me longer than I anticipated to tie-up the loose ends of this fascinating case. But with the invaluable assistance of Chief Inspector Ellis and his officers in Holt, I now have a reasonably clear view of all the key features. Watson, I imagine you are likely to be the only one present who does not know our newly arrived guest – allow me to introduce you to Toby Baxter."

In contrast to the now beaming Chief Inspector Ellis, the thin, ashen-faced Baxter could barely raise a smile as he nodded towards me and then acknowledged both his employer and workmate. Holmes's intervention had expedited his release from detention, but it seemed clear to me that he had been shaken by the news that his father was the killer.

Holmes beckoned for Ellis and Baxter to be seated with the rest of us in the comfortable armchairs scattered around the bay window of the library. He then began to outline what he had discovered.

"This has been something of a convoluted affair. Initially, it looked to be a straightforward enough case. A known poacher comes onto an estate with the intention of taking some gamebirds and is caught by one of the diligent estate workers. In his enthusiasm, the young gamekeeper inadvertently shoots the poacher and imagines – initially, at least – that he can claim to be innocent of the act. But on his return to the body, when confronted with the clear evidence before him, readily confesses to Mr. Aldous that he was in fact the shooter. On the strength of this, he is arrested and finds himself facing a charge of murder.

"Now, there we could have left it. For the evidence of the shotgun, the discarded cartridge and the distinctive boot prints all appeared to support the assertion that Toby Baxter was guilty." At this point, Holmes cast a glance towards the chief inspector, who flushed momentarily. "No doubt, if this case had progressed, any barrister worth his salt would have argued for the charge against Baxter to be reduced to one of manslaughter – still a very serious charge in the circumstances.

"And yet, our case begins to unravel from the start! The shotgun taken from the gamekeeper proves *not* to be the murder weapon, having a firing pin starkly different from that which struck the fatal cartridge. And it is my assertion that the two very distinctive trails of boot prints found at the scene were in fact left by different individuals. One was Toby Baxter's – we know that, because of the testimony of Mr. Aldous. The other set was left by the killer."

It was Chief Inspector Ellis who interjected, no doubt echoing the thoughts of others in the room and being keen to reassert his authority. "I'm sorry, Mr. Holmes, but having eliminated young Baxter, it seems patently obvious who the culprit is. You yourself have provided us with the main evidence against him – the gun, the boots, and the pheasant – and I understand that Mr. Kendrick has now given a statement which provides further crucial testimony. The man who shot Joe Whistlethorpe has to be *Ethan Baxter*. Toby realised it when he saw his father's familiar sealskin cap. Out of misplaced loyalty, he refused to turn his father in and was prepared to take the blame himself."

Holmes nodded slowly and stepped forward towards Toby Baxter. "I have had the advantage of interviewing our young friend here before he was released from his police cell in Holt. When pressed, he confirmed exactly what you have said – that he believed his father to be the shooter and had sought to cover for him. Perhaps you would be good enough to explain why you did this, Toby?"

The former Baker Street Irregular cleared his throat and then spoke in a quiet, but confident voice: "I was proud to get my job on this estate and will be forever grateful to Mr. Holmes, Sir Terence and Mr. Aldous for the faith they had in my abilities. When I returned to Norfolk, I did not expect to encounter my father. All I had known of him previously was that he had left my mother and I when I was only two years of age. My mother had died shortly afterwards and I then went to live with an ageing great aunt in Essex. She cared more for her cattle than she did me, and certainly fed and housed them better. When I was ten, I ran away to London and was taken in by a carter who worked me very hard. But I made some friends of my own age, and then met Mr. Holmes. My life began to improve after that.

"I had only been in Billington for a couple of weeks when I heard from a local farrier that two or three poachers were living in Letheringsett and had been coming onto the estate at night. I took it upon myself to find out what I could and discovered that one of them lived on Hurdle Lane. When I called to confront him and warn him about the consequences of venturing onto the estate again, he laughed and then invited me in, explaining who he was. He had learnt of my appointment and had then seen me on the estate, realising that I had to be his son. He said he was both proud and humbled to learn that his only offspring had achieved such a position in life.

"Despite my misgivings I found myself drawn to the man and began to spend more and more time with him when not at work. He told me that he had once been a gamekeeper himself, on a large estate in the west of the county. There he had met my mother, a servant girl in the big house. His employer had initially taken a dim view of their relationship but had allowed them to marry and live in a cottage on the estate. When I was born, my father had just been promoted to head gamekeeper and his prospects looked good. But then disaster struck. An under-butler on the estate made some advances towards my mother and when my father found out, he set about him, leaving him very badly injured. As well as being ordered off the estate, my father was convicted of the assault and then spent two years in prison. My mother could not stay in the estate cottage and was forced to leave her position. She had apparently travelled around from that point on, finding work wherever she could to support the two of us, but had eventually succumbed to pneumonia. Being incarcerated, my father had been unable to help and when released from prison felt I would be better off continuing to live with my great aunt.

"As we became closer, he agreed not to poach on the Billington Estate and said he would do all he could to stop anyone finding out that we were related. That way we could both carry on in our respective roles. It wasn't ideal but was all I could get him to agree to. In return, I began to help him out with food and rent money. I even gave him one of the two pairs of boots I had bought for my work – the prints of which you now know were found at the plantation. Things continued to improve when he announced that he had found a lodger, a man who could move in and share the rent. This took some of the pressure off me and meant that I did not have to keep visiting the cottage and risking exposure.

"That was how things were until this week, when I went to investigate some shots in the earlier hours of Wednesday morning and discovered the dead body of Joe Whistlethorpe.

I knew he was a poacher, but initially had no idea why anyone would want to shoot him. But when I returned to the body with Mr. Aldous and saw the sealskin cap, I believed I had the answer. Knowing my father would not survive another stretch in prison, I took it upon myself to own up to the shooting. I realise now what a mistake that was."

Holmes then interposed. "Let us turn to Ethan Baxter. When Dr Watson and I visited his cottage this morning we discovered the offending shotgun and the boots which left those very distinctive prints on the Crinkle Crankle Plantation. We also seized the pheasant which had been taken from beneath the body of Whistlethorpe. My examination showed that the wing feathers still had traces of what looked like human blood on them. According to Mr. Kendrick's testimony, Ethan Baxter had been out poaching that fateful night and hated Whistlethorpe. All ways round, the case against Ethan Baxter looks pretty persuasive, yet he is *not* our killer."

There was an explosion of chatter in the room. It took Holmes a few moments to make himself heard: "The killer is a determined, ruthless and capable criminal who has killed before. He carefully planned the murder of Joe Whistlethorpe to rid himself of a much-loathed adversary and deliberately sought to lay the blame at the feet of Ethan Baxter. Is there anything you would like to say in your defence, Mr. Kendrick?"

All eyes turned towards the poacher. William Kendrick retained an air of detached composure and merely grinned at Holmes. "That is some performance, sir! But I am struggling to understand why you would think me guilty. Where is your evidence? Your energies would be better spent trying to trace the whereabouts of Ethan, who has clearly fled after committing the murder."

Holmes responded firmly but dispassionately. "The case against you is overwhelming, and I am certain that your destiny lies at the end of a hangman's noose. Perhaps we should start at the beginning, with your murder of Ethan Baxter..."

Kendrick leapt from his seat with such savagery that I was momentarily unable to act. He lunged towards Holmes with his hands outstretched, teeth bared and eyes aflame. It was Toby Baxter who rose in concert with the man and thwarted the assault. The two police constables then came into their own, each grabbing an arm and resisting Kendrick's attempts to kick himself free. Within minutes they had him pinned to the floor and secured with a sturdy set of police handcuffs. He was then wrestled back into his chair, where he slumped, violet in hue and breathing heavily.

Holmes displayed little reaction to what had just occurred but nodded towards Baxter. "Thank you, Toby. I should explain that in interviewing my young friend in his cell earlier, I was forced to tell him the distressing news about the death of his father at your hands, Mr. Kendrick. He was fully prepared for any stunt you might pull."

It was Sir Terence who now spoke. "My dear Holmes, I must confess to being a little confused at the nature of your revelations. Could you please explain how the death of Ethan Baxter is connected to the shooting of Joe Whistlethorpe?"

I could see that Aldous and Ellis were both nodding their heads in agreement. Holmes then sought to clarify matters. "My apologies, Sir Terence. Let me take you through the pertinent facts. When I had interviewed Toby and arranged for his release, I was told by the custody sergeant that another detainee wished to have a word with me. Lodged in a cell close by was a man called Stephen Matlock. Dr Watson and I had been told about him earlier in the day. He is being held for a violent assault unrelated to this case. Hearing that I was investigating the death of Whistlethorpe, he was keen to share some information with me, explaining that the poacher had been a very close friend of his.

"According to Matlock, the community of poachers in Letheringsett used to meet up regularly. They had a general agreement about which lands they would poach on, and each man had his own recognised 'patch.' But that all changed with the arrival of Kendrick. He moved into the village and began working at a local grain store alongside Ethan Baxter, eventually becoming his lodger. When it became clear that both men enjoyed their night-time pursuits, Kendrick was introduced to the other poachers. But despite their initial friendliness, he refused to stick to their unwritten code of practice and began to poach whenever and wherever he wished. Within weeks, Whistlethorpe and Matlock had declared something approaching a state of war with Kendrick and had made it clear to Baxter that he would have to choose which side he was aligned with. Baxter had apparently pledged his loyalty to them and had agreed to send Kendrick packing."

Kendrick laughed unexpectedly. "Send me packing? He wasn't capable of that, none of them were!"

Holmes gave him a withering look. "No, you were not to be outdone. You'd faced tougher opponents in your time, hadn't you? You try to disguise that West Country accent of yours, but it's easy enough to detect. When I was at the police station in Holt, I sent a telegram to the Chief Constable of the Devon County Constabulary and had a pretty speedy reply. He knew of you – it seems you have quite some form, and not just as a poacher. It was only a year ago that you were released from Dartmoor Prison having served 15 years for killing a gamekeeper."

"What of it, you still can't prove that I killed Ethan or Joe. This is all hot air!"

"Oh, but I can. Your story about Ethan Baxter leaving the house to go poaching was barely plausible. He had no hatred for Whistlethorpe and certainly no motive to kill him. Like his son, Baxter was tidy and methodical. His house bears testimony to that – everything in its place. Are we to believe that he tracked Whistlethorpe, shot him in cold blood, had the composure to pick up the dead pheasant and then *accidentally dropped* his sealskin cap? If he had done so, and had then returned to Hurdle Lane prior to taking flight, why did he leave his boots and shotgun behind? Why would he take the time to hang the pheasant in the pantry? The truth is he was already dead by the time you set out to walk to Billington that night to despatch Whistlethorpe."

"You keep saying that I killed Ethan, but where's the proof?"

"I am something of a stickler for detail, Mr. Kendrick. Did you really imagine that I would miss the tell-tale signs of your deadly fight? Your head, face and hands testify to the severity of the encounter. By all accounts, the man was no pushover. You might remember that I spent some time in your kitchen and garden earlier today. Despite your efforts to clean up, it was easy to discern the small droplets of blood which were sprayed up the wall of the pantry and the small remnants of glass from the bottle you used to bludgeon him to death. The muddy prints along the garden path showed me how you had dragged his lifeless body towards the vegetable patch and the large plot of bare earth more than hinted at his final resting place. You had to dig up about a dozen cabbages to create enough space to bury him and you tossed these behind the shed. After all, you had no need for them – there were already three sitting in a basket within the pantry."

Kendrick looked dumbstruck. He continued to retain his sullen composure but said nothing further as Holmes carried on.

"Inadvertently, you kept referring to Ethan Baxter in the past tense when you gave us an account of your recollections that night. And you knew where everything was placed, as if you had been waiting for someone to call so you could point them in the direction of the gun, the boots, and the gamebird. When Chief Inspector Ellis's men dig over that vegetable patch, I feel certain that my suspicions will be confirmed."

The chief inspector took this as a cue and nodded to PC Peck, who then left the library.

"So, we come to the second killing. When I examined Ethan's boots, I found some small, green, woollen fibres adhering to the leather uppers – the same green wool that I see on your socks today. You thought that by wearing the boots and using Ethan's shotgun you could implicate him in the murder and then claim he had fled to be with his supposed 'lady friend' in Sheringham. Two birds with one stone, eh! You knew Whistlethorpe's routine – where he usually liked to poach – and you sat in wait for him. It was then an easy task to shoot him when he emerged from the woods to retrieve the dead pheasant."

"Bravo, Mr. Holmes!" cried Chief Inspector Ellis. "Your reputation is richly deserved, but I think my men can handle things from here. The sooner we get this man behind bars, the better!" He stood and beckoned to his officers who then began to manhandle Kendrick from the library. The poacher continued to say nothing.

"I could not agree more, Ellis." This time it was Sir Terence who spoke. "Now, Holmes – I hope that you and Dr Watson will accept my hospitality this evening?"

"I am sure that I speak for both of us when I say that we would be delighted to accept. I am told that you keep an excellent cellar and have some vintage claret from the Château Margaux."

"Yes, indeed!" came the reply. He turned towards Aldous. "Isaac, I think it would be fitting if you could also join us. And if you have not already planned a nightshift for him, I would be very pleased to see Mr. Baxter at my table tonight. I am sure that he would welcome a decent meal before he returns to his gamekeeping duties."

Toby Baxter was overcome with emotion and thanked Sir Terence and Mr. Aldous. He then began to express his gratitude for the support he had received from Holmes and I. My colleague would have none of it and silenced him by saying, "It was the least we could do for an honoured member of the Baker Street Irregulars."

I cast a glance outside and into the rose garden of Billington Hall. The first heavy flurries of snow had begun to fall, and the wide expanse of lawn was already carpeted in white. For once it felt good to be away from the incessant hustle and bustle of the capital and the demands of urban life.

6. The Case of the Learned Linguist

In the February of 1923, we all stood aghast at the discoveries made by the Egyptologist Howard Carter. In opening the sealed burial chamber of Tutankhamun, a Pharaoh of the Eighteenth Dynasty of Egypt, the British archaeologist succeeded in stunning the world with the mysteries and magnificence of that early civilisation. And in a strange twist of fate, Sherlock Holmes and I were to be engaged in our own, less celebrated, case of treasure hunting that month, while working in collaboration with the renowned detective Jonathon Pendleton and his esteemed colleague, Dr. Leonard Hooper.

It had been some time since I had seen Holmes. Seemingly content to reside alone with only his beloved bees for company, the sixty-nine-year-old had become something of a recluse on his quiet smallholding on the south coast. Yet he had not given up on his investigative work; every so often he would accept a case which intrigued him and set to work with all the energy and enthusiasm of a man half his age.

That particular morning, I received a wholly unexpected communication from him – a call from a telephone box in the village close to his home. It was only the third or fourth time I had known him to call me, so I imagined it must be important.

"Watson, my good fellow. I trust you and your dear wife are in the best of health? I apologise for the abruptness of the call, but wondered if you might be free at two o'clock today? I recollect that this is the afternoon you usually reserve for a round of golf. Is there any chance I could persuade you to drive out to the South Downs for what promises to be a fascinating case?"

It was an invitation to set my pulse racing; the familiar call to arms that I had missed so much in recent years. I readily agreed to the proposition and, after a light luncheon of ham and baked potatoes, set off from home in my Crossley 20/25.

It was a clear, warm day and as I headed away from the capital was reminded just how idyllic the counties of Surrey and Sussex were. The car responded well on the rolling hills and twists and turns of the narrow lanes leading to Holmes's smallholding. When I arrived, a little after half-past one, my colleague was waiting at the gate, a look of undisguised joy on his face. It was clear that we had both missed each other's company. I left the car pulled up on the verge close to the stone wall of the property and followed Holmes up the steep stony drive.

After some initial pleasantries over a cup of strong tea provided by his housekeeper, we settled in the comfortable and spacious living room of the cottage and Holmes outlined the case he had agreed to take on: "There is a large manor house named *Ramallah*, some three miles north of here, which had, until recently, been occupied by the academic and linguist, Arthur Connolly. His specialist field of study was the oral traditions and early written texts of the major religions. But he also contributed much to the development of the *comparative method* by which the major languages of the world can be systematically grouped with regard to their sounds, grammatical structures, and vocabulary. It has helped us to ascertain which languages are, in a sense, *genealogically* related.

"Connolly was a devoted, but somewhat brusque and difficult, man, who put his academic prowess ahead of his affability. I had an occasion to work with him ten years ago on a case which hinged on the translation of an early Tibetan text. The self-made man was quite brilliant but lacking in any discernible humour. His wife of more than forty years died of consumption shortly afterwards, leaving him to make provision for his three sons, Roger, George, and Colin. I say *make provision*, because he spent so much of his time overseas, accepting visiting lectureships in places like Rome, Venice, and Jerusalem, that he had little time to act as much of a father. Each of the boys was placed in a private boarding school and during their periods of holiday they would return to the manor to be looked after by their diligent housekeeper and the other household staff.

"Some months back, Arthur Connolly suffered a stroke and the doctors determined that he should stop travelling and resign himself to a quiet life back in England. With some reluctance he agreed to do so, and had some adaptations made to his home to accommodate his limited mobility. Alongside his language and theological interests, he had a fascination with electrical devices – his being the first domestic property in the county to have electricity installed. The whole house was filled with the most sophisticated electrical contraptions, many designed and created by the man himself. In his final days he contented himself with his books and machines, leaving home on only one or two occasions to travel north to some spiritual sites in Scotland.

"Six weeks ago, the man passed away. Within the family, it was fully expected that he would leave his property and the bulk of his considerable fortune to his eldest son, Roger. And yet, when the will was read, he surprised all of those present with the provisions he had made. In short, apart from a few specific bequests to academic institutions and his loyal household staff, his sons were left no direct inheritance of any kind."

He paused at that point and reached for his briar pipe and a tin of Peterson's tobacco. I took the opportunity to quiz him on this final revelation. "You say they were left *no direct inheritance*. Does that imply that they were left something on a conditional basis?"

Holmes chuckled as he lit the pipe, taking two or three puffs before responding. "That's the spirit, Watson! I knew I could rely on you to get straight to the nub of the issue. Connolly did make provision for one of the sons to inherit but did not specify which. All his remaining estate was placed in a trust for a period of up to one year. If none of the sons put in a claim during that period, the assets are to be gifted to the Hebrew University of Jerusalem."

"Incredible," I responded. "And what were the conditions of the inheritance?"

He stood at that moment and looked across to the window which afforded a full view of the drive. "That we shall shortly discover. All the information I have shared with you to this point was included in a letter I received from the youngest son, Colin, three days ago. I wrote back to confirm that I would be pleased to meet with him today. That is his small car which is attempting to negotiate the drive. Arthur Connolly clearly loved his linguistic mysteries, for he set his boys a challenge. As I understand it, the first of the three sons to find their father's hidden 'treasure' will inherit everything. Beyond that, I know no more, so I will be as keen as you to hear young Colin's testimony."

The man shown into the study was in his early-twenties; a pale tousle-haired fellow with bright blue eyes and a warm countenance. He could not have been more enthusiastic in greeting the two of us and thanking Holmes for agreeing to see him. "Mr. Holmes, my father was a great admirer of yours, so this is indeed a pleasure. And you, Dr. Watson! I have you to thank for the marvellous detective stories which I read so many times as a child. I had not realised that you would be here!"

For some reason, I felt a tad sensitive at his final remark given my declining years. *Did he actually think I had passed away some time before?* Still, I let the matter rest, seeing that he was eager to share his story. Furnished with a steaming cup of tea, Colin Connolly was invited to reveal the nature of his father's treasure quest.

"Gentlemen. I should start by saying something about my father's obsession with words, language, and belief. You will know of his academic work, but his personal and private life was taken up with puzzles and conundrums and the collection of obscure books on theological topics. While I admired the man, I think I can speak for all three of us, as brothers, in saying that he rarely devoted any real time to being a father. When we were in his company, he would have us translating Latin texts or attempting to unpick anagrams, believing that this would enhance our education. In reality, it turned us against most of the subjects which he laboured so hard to understand and expound upon."

I was building a picture in my mind of a domineering, self-centred, man who would probably have been content to live without children. Colin Connolly's next disclosure did nothing to dissuade me of that thought. "Father was, in every sense, a very controlling man. When each of us came of age and was faced with decisions about which vocation to pursue in life, he sought to exert his influence over our choices. He challenged us to show our affection for him by choosing a suitable academic route into a career like his own. He made it clear that the son who achieved the most in life, by following such a course of action, would eventually inherit most of his estate, adding that *nothing will come of nothing.*

"As the first to face the challenge, Roger did his best to comply. He was studious and hardworking, eventually being offered a place at Oxford University to study theology and classics. When he graduated, father was delighted, but this approval soon waned when he learned that Roger had accepted a job as an English teacher at a school in St Albans. That he also planned to marry a young woman who was the daughter of a steeplejack only added to my father's evident frustration."

Holmes interjected at this point, pointing the stem of his pipe towards our client: "Did your father suggest that this had ruined Roger's likelihood of inheriting?"

Connolly shook his head quickly and pursed his lips. "Not as such. But father's constant refrain whenever we did anything that he did not approve of, was, reconsider *lest you may mar your fortunes.*"

"I see," said Holmes, rather enigmatically, "please do continue."

"My brother George was always the brightest, but from an early age he developed an inherently obstinate trait, which often set him against my father. He accepted a place at Durham University to read English and medieval literature but was sent down in his first year for his constant drunkenness and for running up a sizable gambling debt. Since that time, he has continued to reside in Durham and works as a manager in a carpet factory. For well over a year, my father refused to speak to him, at one point sending George a vindictive letter which said *you have no eyes in your head, nor no money in your purse.* He took it as a clear indication that he had ruined his chances of inheriting."

This time I interposed. "How did your brother react to that?"

"He was furious at first but made every effort to regain my father's trust. He arranged for all the floor coverings in the family home to be replaced by the very best carpets following my father's stoke. It was a gesture that was very well-received and led to a thawing of relations between the two."

"And what of your own story, Mr. Connolly? How did you fare at the hands of your father?" Holmes then asked.

Connolly smiled uneasily. "I had no interest in theology or linguistics, but I did have a fascination for the electrical devices which my father built. When I was twelve years old, we spent some time creating our own Van de Graaff generator. From that moment on, I knew that I wanted to study electrical engineering, and, on leaving school, applied to the Faraday House Electrical Engineering College in Bloomsbury to do just that. My father was livid and said he could not believe I had so little affection and respect for him. Despite my protestations that I admired him greatly and thought he would approve of my choice, he would hear none of it. Nevertheless, I accepted the place I was offered. And, like George, was cast adrift and forced to take a job as an apprentice electrician to fund my college fees."

"That must have been heart wrenching," I exclaimed.

He answered confidently with no apparent malice. "It was at first, but I learned a lot from the experience. My three years at college were rewarding and I made a lot of new friends. Having lived a very sheltered life to that point, it genuinely broadened my horizons. And before my father died, I also had something of a reconciliation with him."

"How so?" inquired Holmes.

"His mobility had been greatly reduced by the stroke and he soon became reliant on the use of a wheelchair. The room where he spent most of his time was the large library on the ground floor, but he insisted on retaining an upstairs bedroom. The household staff would have to carry him and the chair up and down the winding staircase of the house – a not inconsiderable task. The solution was to have an electric lift installed within the library. My father knew that I had the expertise to undertake such a project and asked Roger to contact me. I agreed to the task and within three weeks the team I had assembled had completed all the building work and electrical installation required. When he used it for the first time, my father was reduced to tears; the first time I had ever known him to demonstrate any real emotion. Until he died, we continued to spend time together, although he never acknowledged that he had been wrong to treat Roger, George and myself the way he did."

"Indeed," said Holmes. "So, now we come to the matter of the will and the inheritance. What was the nature of the challenge you were set?"

Connolly took a deep breath and shook his head. "It was a final reminder of the man's controlling nature. Even beyond the grave he has sought to taunt us with his parlour games. The will specified that he had a secret hidden 'treasure' but did not say what this was. The only clue to its whereabouts was a curious word square which I will share with you shortly. Each of us was given a copy. Along the bottom of the sheet ran his familiar phrase *nothing will come of nothing*. The first of us to locate this treasure will presumably benefit from it, but will also inherit the residual estate, which must not be shared between us. It is a challenge designed to set brother against brother."

"And has that happened?" I uttered.

"Not exactly. George has continued to live beyond his means and his last hope was that father might leave him a small legacy sufficient to pay off some, or all, of his debts. As that hasn't happened, he has withdrawn completely and refuses to even contemplate the challenge. Roger spent a month trying to make sense of the square, but ultimately gave up, saying that I was welcome to the treasure if I could locate it. I too have spent many hours trying to unravel the mystery but know my limitations. Recognising your expertise, Mr. Holmes, I believed you to be the best person to consult. I am determined to put the matter to rest."

Holmes beamed. "As am I! I would be delighted to accept your commission and I'm sure that Dr. Watson will be equally pleased to assist. But we must have the information! As yet, you have not shared with us the enigmatic *word square* that you alluded to."

Connolly's face flushed and he apologised quickly. Reaching for an inside pocket he withdrew a piece of foolscap and passed it to Holmes. My colleague jumped up and spread the sheet out on a table before the window, inviting me to join him in examining it. On the sheet was printed the following:

P	E	A	C	E
E	N	T	E	R
A	T	L	A	S
C	E	A	S	E
E	R	S	E	S

"Most interesting," he intoned. "Any thoughts, Watson?"

I studied the words most intently but could see no obvious logic or pattern beyond the fact that each word ran both across and down the square. I had to acknowledge as much.

Holmes turned back to Connolly: "Did you or Roger make any progress in deciphering the square?"

"No. Roger was convinced that the word 'Atlas' was significant. There is a large atlas in the library at *Ramallah*, but though we looked, neither of us could find anything in it. Similarly, from his studies, Roger believed that 'Erses' most likely referred to one of the several related languages of the Celts. Father had a stone folly in the grounds of the house on which was written *An Tiarna leat* – the Gaelic for 'The Lord be with you.' My brother spent a considerable amount of money having large sections of the soil around the folly excavated, convinced that the treasure lay hidden beneath. Later, in desperation, he also had the folly dismantled, brick by brick, yet still found nothing."

"I see," replied Holmes. "Well, we should start with a visit to *Ramallah* to see if any further clues can be found on this treasure hunt. If Dr. Watson is agreeable, we will follow you by car back to your former home. It would seem to be the logical first step in our endeavours."

****

The drive north took longer than I expected, for though it was but three miles, the route took us along four or five lanes which were little more than tumbril tracks. Connolly seemed to have scant regard for the suspension of his car, but I winced each time my Crossley lurched in response to the uneven ground. When at last we reached the entrance gate to the manor house, I was reassured to see that the half-mile drive to the property had a tarmacadam surface. It was the smoothest stretch of road I had encountered since leaving London.

Ramallah was a magnificent property created in the Jacobean style. While additional wings had been added to the back of the house in later centuries, the plan and elevation of the main building looked largely unchanged from its original Elizabethan construction. Within the house were ornamental carvings, columns, and pilasters, while outside there were turreted Tudor-style wings at either end with large mullioned windows.

On our arrival, we were greeted by a sturdy, grey-haired woman, whom Colin Connolly introduced as Mrs. Trimble, the housekeeper. It was clear that the two had a great deal of affection for each other, for the woman embraced him as if he were a favourite nephew or a cherished grandchild. Mrs. Trimble proved to be friendly and amenable throughout our visit and insisted that we partake of some tea and Victoria sponge cake in the kitchen before being shown around the property.

By far the largest room in the house was the library which had been created by Arthur Connolly. The long rectangular room housed many thousands of books and manuscripts, which sat within exquisitely carved bookcases running around three of its walls. Alongside religious and linguistic texts of all descriptions, there were early bound volumes by luminaries such as Jonathan Swift, Christopher Marlowe, William Shakespeare, and John Milton. The fourth wall was lined with oak panels, some of which had been decorated with paintings of animals, birds, and trees. Down the centre of the room, tables and chairs had been placed at intervals and on some sat odd-looking electrical devices which I imagined to be some of the contraptions that the deceased man had been so fond of.

The property felt more like a museum than a family home and did nothing to change my opinion of the academic who had furnished it. It was a cold and unwelcoming interior lacking any familial touches and revealing nothing of the three young men who had once grown up there.

Having walked around all the principal areas of the building, Holmes seemed content to return to the library. He invited Connolly and I to sit and announced suddenly, "This is where we shall find our next clue." He then addressed our client directly: "For this seems to be the epicentre of all that your father held dear."

He withdrew the folded foolscap from his pocket and regarded it once more. "Let us start with the first word, 'Peace.' An obscure word, perhaps, but one that is often cited in religious and spiritual contexts. Symbolic depictions of peace in the Christian traditions of ancient Greece often included olive branches and doves. And if we look towards the oak panelling on our left, we can see that one particular panel is painted with both – for the dove is clearly holding within its painted beak the sprig of an olive tree.

"The second word in the square invites us to 'Enter.' He moved towards the wall and placed his hand in the centre of the oak panel. With a gentle push, the panel opened as a result of a hidden spring-release mechanism to reveal a cavity behind the wall. Connolly looked on incredulously as Holmes reached into the space to remove a second sheet of folded foolscap.

"Amazing, Mr. Holmes! What does it say?"

"Well, it continues the quest, for there is a further word square. But we are clearly on the right path, for the adage along the bottom of the sheet reads *to thee and thine, hereditary forever*. He walked across to us and spread the sheet out on a small table. Connolly and I shifted our chairs to view the document. In the middle of the paper was printed the following:

F	A	R	A	D
A	R	O	M	A
R	O	T	O	R
A	M	O	R	A
D	A	R	A	F

I was the first to comment. "This one seems even more obscure than the first. I'm glad that you were able to make sense of the previous square, Holmes. Do you have any thoughts on this?"

My colleague was scrutinising the sheet with considerable intensity. Connolly and I waited for him to respond, both anticipating that he would have a ready answer, but he replied in the negative. "At this stage, gentlemen, I have to say that I have not the faintest clue as to its meaning. 'Aroma' is too general without context, and the words 'Farad' and 'Daraf' are completely new to me. I believe 'Amora' to be of Hebrew origin but will need to consult with an expert to verify its significance. We clearly have more work to do on this one, but I know a man who might assist us."

Somewhat unexpectedly, Connolly interjected with evident enthusiasm. "Mr. Holmes, I think I can help to unravel at least part of the mystery. As an electrical engineer, I know that a 'Farad' is a measure of electrical capacitance. The term was originally devised by Latimer Clark and Charles Bright in the early 1860s in honour of the English scientist Michael Faraday. In 1881, it was officially adopted by the International Congress of Electricians in Paris as a unit of electrical capacitance. A 'Daraf' is a reciprocal measure of electrical elastance, the inverse of capacitance, hence the reversal of the word 'Farad'. It was coined by the Irish-American electrical engineer Arthur E. Kennelly two or three years back."

Holmes was ecstatic in his response. "Your specialist knowledge is exemplary. I'm not sure I fully understand what *capacitance* and *elastance* are, but I am privileged to be in the company of a man who does! Now, look again at the square. Does anything else suggest itself to you?"

Connolly looked down once more. His face then lit up for a second time. "Indeed. The reference to the word 'Rotor', alongside the other two words, would suggest to me that we are looking for some sort of motor. A rotor is the rotating component of an electromagnetic system which drives an electric motor."

"Splendid!" I exclaimed. "Well, there are plenty of electrical contrivances around us. Perhaps one of them holds the key to this quest."

Holmes was not so sure. "You have unpicked a major part of this second word square, Mr. Connolly, but we still have some way to go, I fear. Let us leave the wording of this for the moment and return to our first square." He placed the original sheet down beside the second. "We have ascertained the relevance of the first two words, but now come to both 'Atlas' and 'Cease.' Is it suggesting that an atlas is our endpoint in solving this particular part of the quest? And what of 'Erses'?"

He turned and began to scan the rows of bookshelves, before quizzing Connolly once more. "You mentioned earlier that the library contains a large atlas. Could you locate it for me?"

Our client rose and headed towards one of the bookshelves on the far wall of the library. Opening a large glass door, he retrieved a sizeable tome from the shelf and brought it back to Holmes who wasted no time in setting it down on the table and turning to the contents page. "An 1895 copy of *The Times Survey Atlas of the World*. A magnificent book. Now let us see what we can find in the maps relating to Scotland."

Connolly expressed some surprise. "Roger and I spent some time going through each page of that atlas but found nothing. Why do you believe the geography of Scotland to be of particular interest?"

"The word 'Erses' relates to the Gaelic language of the Celts as the two of you had established, but is most often associated with *Scottish* Gaelic." He turned to a section of the atlas and then retrieved a magnifying glass from an outside pocket. As I had seen him do many hundreds of times on previous cases, he then stooped and began to examine every inch of the page. After some seconds he withdrew from the atlas and let out an exclamation: "I believe I have it! If you look closely at the small hamlet of 'Barkip' in North Ayrshire, you will see that beside it is written in the smallest of characters two additional words – 'Lollard House'."

"But what does it mean?" I asked.

"That we have yet to discover. However, in making sense of both that and the second word square, I believe that a consultation with our good friend Jonathon Pendleton might be in order. You will remember, Watson, that he is something of an expert in ancient religions and occult lore. If anyone can shed light on the words 'Amora' and 'Lollard House,' it is bound to be he. With Mr. Connolly's permission I will see if I can reach him by telephone and arrange a visit this evening."

Connolly had no objection and indicated that Mrs. Trimble would be able to direct him towards the telephone which was in a room off the main entrance lobby. Holmes was gone for a good fifteen minutes and returned with a satisfied look on his face. "That was very productive. Pendleton said it would be easier for him to meet me at my own cottage, as he and Dr. Hooper already have an appointment on the south coast tomorrow and are planning to stay in Brighton tonight. They are to swing by around eight o'clock this evening. If you fancied an overnight stop, there is always the spare room."

"Excellent!" said I. "Having already anticipated such a move, I have my travelling case in the car. I will just need to put in a call back home before we leave here."

"Then we are set." He turned towards our client. "Oh, Mr. Connolly. I also took the opportunity to question Mrs. Trimble about your father's travels in the final weeks of his life. You may remember in your original letter that you alluded to some journeys he had made to Scotland to visit spiritual sites."

"That's correct. He was gone for no more than a few days each time, on a couple of occasions, although I cannot recollect that he ever shared with me where he had gone."

"Well, we could have saved ourselves a little bit of legwork if we had taken the trouble to consult with the capable Mrs. Trimble at an earlier stage. She has just confirmed that on the two occasions Arthur Connolly travelled to Scotland, he stayed with your former butler, Charles Kenyon, at his home in Ayrshire. When he retired two years ago, Kenyon was able to buy a small property *on the outskirts of Barkip*. We have succeeded in unpicking another thread of this very tangled skein!"

It was nearing five-thirty that afternoon when we left the manor house. Holmes agreed to keep Connolly informed of our progress with a call the following day. It did not take us too long to retrace our steps to Holmes's cottage as I managed to find a more direct route back. Within fifteen minutes of our arrival, we were tucking into a fish pie which the housekeeper had prepared in our absence. Seated across the table from the great detective with a glass of locally brewed ale in my hand it felt good to be back in the game.

****

Jonathon Pendleton and Dr. Leonard Hooper were as good as their word, pulling up at the gate of the cottage a little before eight o'clock that evening. Holmes and I walked down the drive to meet them. After some warm greetings and frantic hand shaking, we strolled back towards the cottage. While Holmes was sharing with Pendleton his plans for expanding the number of beehives at the back of the property, Hooper was regaling me with the features of his newly acquired Triumph 10/20. He said that with its 1,400 cc four-cylinder side-valve engine, the car had a top speed of 52 miles per hour and could do around 40 miles to the gallon. I could not fail to be impressed.

We sat in front of a warming fire in the living room as Holmes took the two men through every aspect of the case as he understood it. The two detectives smoked pipes filled with some abominable shag tobacco that Pendleton had brought with him, while Hooper and I both opted for some strong Panamanian cigars. Pendleton was slightly more thickset than I had remembered him being, but his keen dark eyes were as mesmerising as ever. Hooper, in contrast, looked to have lost weight and had distinct shading beneath his eyes, no doubt the result of his workload as a busy medical practitioner.

When we began to re-examine the second word square, Pendleton's specialist knowledge came into its own. "I am not surprised that Arthur Connolly produced the word square in this format. It is known as a *Sator Square,* the original of which ran as follows." He sketched out the wording as I have reproduced it below:

S	A	T	O	R
A	R	E	P	O
T	E	N	E	T
O	P	E	R	A
R	O	T	A	S

"The square is palindromic in every sense, and can be read top-to-bottom, bottom-to-top, left-to-right and right-to-left. It has been found in many parts of the world carved on stone tablets or pressed into clay, the earliest known being found in the ruins of Pompeii, at Herculaneum, where it was buried in the ash of Mount Vesuvius. Other excavations have uncovered similar squares in Rome, Cirencester, and Dura-Europos in Syria.

"There are numerous early Christian associations with the square, with many believing that it was used as a covert symbol for oppressed believers to communicate their presence to each other. Interpretations of the words and letters are also many and varied. It is possible to form a Greek cross by repositioning the letters around the central letter 'N' to read 'Pater Noster' in Latin - or *Our Father* - vertically and horizontally. The remaining letters – two lots of 'A' and 'O' – are believed to represent *Alpha* and *Omega*, which further reference the omnipresence of God. And in *The Coptic Prayer of the Virgin in Bartos*, Christ is described as crucified with five nails, named 'Sator,' 'Arepo,' 'Tenet,' 'Opera' and 'Rotas.' So, for Arthur Connolly this would have been a significant linguistic creation."

Holmes was fascinated. "But what of this word 'Amora' in Connolly's own square? Am I right in saying that it is of Hebrew origin?"

Pendleton smiled. "Yes, it originates from the Hebrew word āmōrā, meaning *interpreter*. 'Amora' is the singular for a group of Jewish scholars known as the *Amoraim* who were active in the rabbinical academies of Galilee and Babylonia from the third to the sixth centuries. The word effectively translates as *those who say*, what we might describe in a modern sense as *spokesmen*. These scholars gave commentaries on – and interpretations of – the early oral traditions of Judaism, including religious law and theology, before these were written down as texts. The latter comprise the *Mishnah* – a written compendium of the original oral law – and the *Gemara*, the recorded interpretations of those early scholars. Together, they make up the *Talmud* which is the central written text of Rabbinic Judaism."

Hooper seemed a little sceptical. "Is there any chance that we are reading a little too much into all of this? Could it be that Connolly just needed a convenient word to fit the complex structure of his square and plumped for the word 'Amora' simply because it fit with the real words he wanted to convey?"

Both detectives looked reflective, but it was Holmes who answered first: "It is quite possible, of course, but from what we have learned thus far, it is quite clear that Connolly was a clever man who chose his words with absolute precision. Given his academic interests, I cannot see the inclusion of the word as being anything other than a significant clue as to the whereabouts or nature of his hidden treasure."

Pendleton was inclined to agree but acknowledged that we should keep an open mind. Holmes then asked him about the words 'Lollard House' which had been written in the atlas. While both agreed that this was likely to be the name of Charles Kenyon's property, Pendleton explained the context. "The Lollards were a religious movement influenced by the early thinking of the English Reformation and the establishment of the Protestant faith. Their beliefs were based on the ideas of John Wycliffe, who was one of the first theologians to translate the Bible into English. The early Lollards – or 'poor priests' – challenged many of the practices and beliefs of the established church and demanded social reform. As a result, many faced persecution for what was seen as heresy. Scotland had its fair share of Lollard families, and there were sizeable numbers in Fife and the districts of Kyle and Carrick, in Ayrshire."

"Once again, we appear to be on the right path!" replied Holmes.

"Indeed." Pendleton then turned to the matter of how to proceed and cast a cheeky glance at Holmes. "I'm taking it that a trip to the house in Barkip is now on the cards – a journey that you would prefer Hooper and I to undertake?"

Holmes laughed heartily and having set down his pipe on a table to his side, rose and stepped across to a large oak cabinet on the right of the hearth. "There is no fooling a true detective," he said, opening the front leaf of the cabinet to reveal a dozen or more bottles of spirits. "I had at least thought to ply you with a decent Scotch or a warming glass of brandy before making the request! I have something of a busy schedule already this week, for I am due to meet with the Commissioner of the Metropolitan Force on Thursday to discuss a European bank fraud which has ramifications for fifteen peers of the realm."

Pendleton took this in good spirit and seemed keen to assist his close colleague. "I would be delighted to pursue this further if Hooper can spare a little more of his time. We are already due to wrap up a kidnapping case in Brighton tomorrow morning but could make the journey north on Wednesday."

Hooper voiced no objection and said that the journey would give him a chance to fully run in his new car. Both men seemed delighted at the prospect of teaming up again as we had done on many occasions in the past. And as Holmes did not possess a telephone, it was agreed that Hooper would keep in touch with me as the case developed. A short while later we said our goodbyes and waved the pair off at the gate by the light from our electric torches.

****

Having driven back home the following morning, I busied myself in the garden for the remainder of the day. And on the Wednesday was called to attend a meeting of my local cricket club who had appointed me as the treasurer some months previously. Later that evening, I received a telephone call from Dr. Hooper to say that they had arrived in Scotland after a journey of more than twelve hours and were to spend the night at a hotel in Ayr. He explained that Holmes had called Colin Connolly first thing that morning and had asked him to drive into London so that he might join the pair on the trip north. All three were to venture across to Barkip the following day. Asked how the car had fared, Hooper was ebullient: "It ran like a dream!"

The following evening my wife and I attended our regular bridge night and did not arrive back home until eleven-thirty. I imagined that Hooper might have tried to call me while we were out, but was optimistic that if there were any news, he would call the next morning. As it transpired, I received no call, but was surprised to receive a letter from him in the first post:

The Old Racehorse Hotel
2 Victoria Park
Ayr
Scotland

Thursday, 8th February, 1923

Dear Dr. Watson,

I hope this finds you well. I tried to call you on the telephone a couple of times today but had no luck. Knowing that we would be travelling back to London first thing on Friday, I thought it best to write to you about all that we have discovered. The postal service from Scotland runs overnight by train to London so you will be receiving this communication many hours before we are likely to reach home!

We've had a pleasant and successful excursion. Connolly has proved to be great company and extremely useful in helping us to find another word square! More of that in a while.

Barkip, which many of the locals refer to as 'The Den,' is a delightfully picturesque hamlet in North Ayrshire, a couple of miles from the town of Beith. The colloquial name seems very apt, for the settlement does indeed sit in a hollow between some magnificent hills. The roads in the area are a little chaotic, mainly used by agricultural traffic and difficult to navigate at any speed.

Pendleton was keen for us to be up early, so that we might have plenty of time to locate Charles Kenyon's property. He needn't have worried, because we found *Lollard House* on the approach to the village – it was clearly signposted off to the left and located at the end of a half-mile track.

Charles Kenyon proved to be an extremely affable fellow and was delighted to see young Connolly. It had apparently been some years since the two had last been together. We were invited in and shown every courtesy by the former butler, who provided us with a most delicious luncheon, including some Highland venison, neeps, and tatties! He did not seem at all surprised that we had called in on him to ask about Arthur Connolly, which suggested that he knew something of the treasure quest. It was clear to us that there was more to be discovered at *Lollard House*.

The house itself is stone-built and dates from the fourteenth century. While small, it is solid and has several similarly robust outbuildings. Asked about its name, Kenyon explained that it had once been the home of Robert Nisbet, a follower of a group known as the "Kyle Lollards." In 1494, 30 of the group were summoned by the Archbishop of Glasgow to be brought before King James IV on a charge of heresy, although the charges against them were eventually dismissed. Nisbet escaped the interrogation but lived in fear of arrest for some years afterwards.

We were a little stunned to learn that the house was originally purchased by Arthur Connolly, who agreed to sell it to Kenyon for something of a peppercorn amount when the butler announced he wished to retire. The academic had apparently researched its history and believed that it might contain something of value (Kenyon knew not what this could be). In the event, he failed to find whatever he had been looking for and had no further use for the house.

The information proved to be crucial. Pendleton pointed out that the first man to translate the *New Testament* into Scots, the indigenous lowland language derived from northern Middle English, was a Murdoch Nisbet. Had Robert Nisbet been a close relative of the man he wondered? If so, he would certainly have feared for his life. Given that Robert Nisbet had avoided arrest on the heresy charge, Pendleton surmised that the property might well contain some sort of "priest hole" in which he had been able to secrete himself. Furthermore, when the Lollards had circulated copies of the newly translated Bible, could this same hideaway have been used to store a copy of the unauthorised text? This would account for Arthur Connolly's interest in the property – a surviving and intact copy of the Bible would be extremely sought after.

We then turned back to the word square found at *Ramallah*. Pendleton focussed on the neglected word 'aroma' as we began to examine the interior and exterior of the house and outbuildings. He postulated that the word implied a smell that was fragrant rather than unpleasant. As a clue, the smell would also have to be one which could be detected all year round – rather than the seasonal nectar of a flowering plant, for example – as Arthur Connolly could not be sure when one of the brothers might attempt to unravel the mystery. With this thought, we approached one of the smaller outbuildings which had a large rosemary bush planted to the left of its door. The aroma of the plant was undeniable!

Pushing open the door, we found ourselves in a space no bigger than ten feet square, on the floor of which were old flagstones set in an uneven pattern before us. It was young Connolly who provided the next clue. He had already noticed that some electrical cabling ran down the far wall and a heavy industrial switch was located in one corner. Given his earlier view that the words 'Farad,' 'Daraf' and 'Rotor' hinted at some sort of electrical motor, he stepped across to the wall and flicked the switch. There was a loud whirring noise from beneath our feet and the jaw-grinding noise of stone passing across stone. And before our eyes one of the flagstones slid slowly beneath another to reveal an opening some twenty inches square!

The priest hole was revealed to be an underground chamber sufficient to hold only one person. As the smallest and most eager of us to investigate, Connolly dropped down into the space and shouted up immediately that he could see the workings of an electro-magnetic motor, which he felt certain had been installed by his father, for it was similar to those used to automatically open the glass roofs of the greenhouses at *Ramallah*. A minute or so later he emerged from the hole with a broad smile, clutching a small metal box.

The third word square was found on a sheet within the box, together with a line running along the bottom edge which read *dearer than eyesight, space, and liberty*. The square was set out as follows:

C	R	I	M	E
R	A	M	A	L
I	M	A	G	E
M	A	G	I	C
E	L	E	C	T

I will not go into any further detail at this stage as to Pendleton's thoughts on its meaning. He was, however, fully convinced that *Lollard House* held no further clues, and our next port of call should be a return to the manor house, hinted at by the word 'Ramal.' For while the word is related to the adjective *ramus*, meaning the branch or twig of a plant, and he believes that it hints at the necessary detour to Scotland, he thinks it signifies more specifically that need to return to *Ramallah*.

We will be setting off from the hotel at first light tomorrow, to make it back in good time. While we will stop off in London to freshen up and enable Connolly to reclaim his car, Pendleton has suggested that if it is convenient for both you and Holmes, we should all plan to meet at *Ramallah* in the evening, around eight o'clock. If that is not convenient for some reason, please leave a message with my locum at the surgery.

I remain, yours sincerely,

Dr. Leonard Hooper

I was overjoyed that they had made such rapid progress on the case and knew that Holmes would be delighted. It was just as well, for as we travelled down from London to meet with our colleagues, he indicated that the meeting with the Police Commissioner at Scotland Yard had not gone well when he had disclosed that as a result of his investigations three of the fifteen peers touched by the bank fraud scandal had been found to be actively complicit in the crime.

When we arrived at *Ramallah*, we were given a very warm welcome by Mrs. Trimble who took our hats and coats and escorted us into the dining room of the house. Colin Connolly had arranged for us to dine in some style as we discussed the significance of what had been discovered in Scotland. Both Pendleton and Connolly were distinctly upbeat as they recounted the discovery of the priest hole. Dr. Hooper looked a little shell-shocked, and I imagined that the many hours of driving over the previous three days had finally taken its toll.

Over coffee, we turned our attention towards the third word square and it was Pendleton who then suggested that we should regroup in the library. Holmes was strongly supportive of the idea and when we had relocated with our beverages, took a seat alongside the rest of us and allowed Pendleton to take the lead.

The lean detective stood in the centre of the room and pointed to the sheet of foolscap. "There is huge significance in the choice of this word 'Crime'. In fact, I will have to apologise in advance to Colin here, for what I am about to say about his father."

Colin smiled and shrugged off the comment: "You must reveal the truth, Mr. Pendleton. That is all I ask."

"My inclination is to believe that Arthur Connolly's hidden treasure is almost certainly a stolen relic or religious artefact, most likely a sacred text of some kind. This library is proof of his obsession. I don't know the provenance of all the printed works within this room but recognise that a great many are not only rare but may be unique. It begs the question, how did an academic on no great salary, lecturing on an obscure range of topics, manage to amass so much wealth? There must have been some skulduggery along the way.

"Our interpretation of the second word, 'Ramal', has once again brought us to the manor house and this room in particular. It is the space which meant most to the academic. 'Image' suggests illumination of some kind, and 'Magic' hints at illusion or some sleight-of-hand. But taken together, I was inclined to believe that the words were pointing us towards one of the devices in this room, namely the *magic lantern*. You will see that we have two examples close by."

He pointed towards a first, which sat on a small table to his left. "An early model, possibly from the eighteenth century, which is illuminated using an oil lamp. However, the lantern on the larger table towards the far wall is more interesting."

He stepped across to the table and pointed at a slightly larger machine. "This lantern is illuminated by an electric light bulb, and I would venture that the electrical apparatus within it was installed by Arthur Connolly himself. Now, I have already ascertained that both machines contain a single glass lantern slide ready for projection. The final word in the square is 'Elect.' It is asking the seeker to *choose* or *decide*. I would be inclined to choose the electric lantern in any case, but the word leaves us in no doubt, for it forms the initial letters of the word *elect*ricity.

"As with so many of the clues set by Arthur Connolly, these have been designed to favour you, Colin, as the youngest son. It can be no coincidence that you were the most likely to unravel the meaning of words such as 'Farad,' 'Daraf,' 'Rotor' and 'Elect.' You were also more likely to be drawn to the electric lantern. I believe that your father only ever wanted you to inherit after his death, for he knew he had done you the greatest injustice in casting you adrift, when all you had done was pursue an interest that he himself shared."

Colin Connolly looked close to tears as he listened to this, but Pendleton continued. "So now I believe we can reveal the nature of the treasure that we have all been seeking." He picked up the electric cable which sat beside the magic lantern and stooped below the table to enable him to plug the machine into a socket on the wall. Having done so, he then flipped a switch on the back of the lantern and illuminated the machine. The lens was positioned to project onto a piece of white panelling beneath one of the bookshelves. The image which appeared, in large black capital letters, was the single word "TALMUD."

Holmes stood up and began to clap rapturously. In turn, we all did the same. It had been a brilliant performance. But young Connolly still looked somewhat confused. After some seconds he asked Pendleton to explain what it meant. The detective obliged him.

"You revealed to Mr. Holmes in the initial stages of this investigation that your father had spent some time in Rome, Venice and Jerusalem. The inclusion of the Hebrew word 'Amora' in the second word square and the reference to Venice piqued my interest. I should explain that the oldest full manuscript of the *Talmud* – the central text of rabbinic Judaism – is one which was printed in Munich in 1342. But a complete printed edition of what is known as the *Babylonian Talmud* was produced in Venice in 1520 by a man named Daniel Bomberg. He was permitted to print the text under the protection of Pope Leo X. Copies of this text are extremely rare and exceedingly valuable. Eight years ago, one was stolen from a private collection in Venice. The authorities failed to catch the thief. Your father was in the city during the time of the theft. I believe it was he who stole the document and smuggled it back to England."

Connolly still looked a little baffled. "So, are you suggesting that this rare manuscript is to be found within this library?"

Pendleton looked triumphant. "Yes. It is the only explanation which fits the facts."

"Then where is it?" countered Connolly politely. "Roger and I spent some time looking at all of the titles in this room in our quest to find a second atlas, when we could find no clues in the one that Mr. Holmes examined. I am certain that we did not come across any title that points towards this *Talmud*."

"That is because the text is very well hidden. In fact, it is the very reason that your father was able to smuggle it out of Venice without being detained. Perhaps Mr. Holmes would like to explain?"

Holmes seemed rather surprised to be asked to reveal the location of the *Talmud* at this juncture. For a brief second, I wondered if this were a ruse on Pendleton's part to test whether the great detective had deduced all that he had but discounted the thought. If there were clues to point to its location, I knew that Holmes would not disappoint.

"Thank you, Pendleton. The answer of course lies in your father's choice of phrase. You see, from the start, we were given clues as to what I imagine must have been one of your father's favourite works of fiction: *nothing will come of nothing; lest you may mar your fortunes; to thee and thine, hereditary forever.* They were consistently drawn from the same work, namely William Shakespeare's *King Lear*. A tragedy in which a King bequeaths his wealth and power to two of his three daughters, having asked each of them to declare their affection for him. The youngest of his offspring refuses to do so and is disinherited because of the man's fatal pride. It is only with his declining health and spiralling insanity that the king realises the mistake he has made.

"As Pendleton indicated earlier, your father clearly realised his own mistake, but did not feel able to disinherit Roger and George. He knew that you were the most likely to solve the treasure quest given the clues he had set. As such, you would then rightly claim the inheritance. Even if you had struggled, he knew you were the only one likely to ask for help. After all, there was nothing to prevent Roger or George seeking some external assistance.

"In order to steal the *Talmud* and keep it hidden within this library, your father arranged for the manuscript to be bound within the leather covers of another book. A little further along the room on the left, is a section devoted to the works of William Shakespeare. Contained within that section is a leather spine which purports to be the play, *King Lear*. In reality, I believe it to be the stolen *Talmud*."

It was Holmes's turn to be applauded and a short while later we retrieved the text from the shelf to confirm all that he and Pendleton had deduced. We marvelled at the condition of the document and could only wonder at its rich history and inherent value. Our thoughts then turned to the question of Colin Connolly's inheritance claim.

"With our assistance, you should have no problem convincing the solicitors of the trust fund that you have successfully located your father's 'treasure' and should therefore inherit all that he left," said Holmes.

Connolly shook his head slowly. "To be honest, gentlemen, I am rather sickened that the object of our quest should be a magnificent sacred text which was obtained in such a despicable fashion. I will put in my claim but will arrange for the *Talmud* to be returned to Venice at the first opportunity. I will also do my best to ascertain that there are no other stolen artefacts in the room. As for the house, while I will not be permitted to share it with my brothers, there is nothing to prevent me from selling it at a later stage and giving them a share of the proceeds. I think that only fair."

"Bravo!" cried Hooper, who stepped across to shake Connolly by the hand. "You are a fine fellow. And by your actions you can help to reverse some of the injustices perpetrated by your father."

Holmes echoed the thought: "That, we can all agree on. Your destiny lies in your own hands now, beyond the parlour games of your father. We wish you every success!"

We left *Ramallah* a short while after. Some weeks later we were called to attend a meeting with the solicitors of Arthur Connolly's trust fund, where it was confirmed that young Colin had been successful in his inheritance claim. It had been one of the most satisfying cases that Holmes and Pendleton had ever worked on together, but it would not be the last. Shortly afterwards they were engaged in *The Adventure of the Purloined Pistol*. But that, as you might surmise, is a story for another day…

About the Author

Mark Mower is a crime writer and historian whose passion for tales about Sherlock Holmes and Dr. Watson began at the age of twelve, when he watched an early black and white film featuring the unrivalled screen pairing of Basil Rathbone and Nigel Bruce. Hastily seeking out the original stories of Sir Arthur Conan Doyle, and continually searching for further film and television adaptations, his has been a lifelong obsession. Now a member of the Crime Writers' Association, the Sherlock Holmes Society of London and the Solar Pons Society of London, he has written numerous crime books.

Mark has contributed to more than 20 Holmes anthologies, including 14 parts of *The MX Book of New Sherlock Holmes Stories*, *The Book of Extraordinary New Sherlock Holmes Stories* (Mango Publishing) and *Sherlock Holmes – Before Baker Street* (Belanger Books). His own books include *A Farewell to Baker Street, Sherlock Holmes: The Baker Street Case-Files, Sherlock Holmes: The Baker Street Legacy* and *Sherlock Holmes: The Baker Street Epilogue* (all with MX Publishing).

Mark's non-fiction titles include *Zeppelin Over Suffolk: The Final Raid of the L48* (Pen & Sword Books); *Bloody British History: Norwich* (The History Press); and *Foul Deeds and Suspicious Deaths in Suffolk* (Wharncliffe Books). His essays have appeared in more than 30 publications, including *Mobile Holmes: Transportation in The Sherlockian Canon* (Baker Street Irregulars) and *Truly Criminal: A Crime Writers' Association Anthology of True Crime* (The History Press).

Copyright Information

"A Diplomatic Affair" ©2019 by Mark Mower. All rights reserved. First published in *Sherlock Holmes and Dr. Watson: The Early Years, Volume II* (Belanger Books, 2019).

"The Neckar Reawakening" ©2021 by Mark Mower. All rights reserved. A different version of this story was first published in letter format on the website *DearHolmes.com* during March 2022.

"The Yuletide Heist" ©2021 by Mark Mower. All rights reserved. First published in *The MX Book of New Sherlock Holmes Stories - Part XXVIII: More Christmas Adventures, 1869-1888* (MX Publishing, 2021).

"The Case of the SS Bokhara" ©2019 by Mark Mower. All rights reserved. First published in *The MX Book of New Sherlock Holmes Stories - Part XX: 2020 Annual, 1891-1897* (MX Publishing, 2020).

"The Misadventure of the Norfolk Poacher" ©2019 by Mark Mower. All rights reserved. First published as a Solar Pons story in *The New Adventures of Solar Pons* (Belanger Books, 2019).

"The Case of the Learned Linguist" ©2021 by Mark Mower. All rights reserved. First published as a Sherlock Holmes and Solar Pons story in *The Meeting of the Minds: The Cases of Sherlock Holmes and Solar Pons, Volume II* (Belanger Books, 2021).